CW00455628

Anonymous

Transactions of the Thirty-First Annual Meeting of the Ohio State Medical Society

Anatiposi

Anonymous

Transactions of the Thirty-First Annual Meeting of the Ohio State Medical Society

Reprint of the original, first published in 1875.

1st Edition 2024 | ISBN: 978-3-38283-100-4

Anatiposi Verlag is an imprint of Outlook Verlagsgesellschaft mbH.

Verlag (Publisher): Outlook Verlag GmbH, Zeilweg 44, 60439 Frankfurt, Deutschland
Vertretungsberechtigt (Authorized to represent): E. Roepke, Zeilweg 44, 60439 Frankfurt, Deutschland
Druck (Print): Books on Demand GmbH, In de Tarpen 42, 22848 Norderstedt, Deutschland

TRANSACTIONS

OF THE

THIRTY-FIRST ANNUAL MEETING

OF THE

Ohio State Medical Society

HELD AT

PUT-IN-BAY,

JUNE 20th, 21st, and 22d, 1876.

—————o—————

CINCINNATI:

A. H. POUNSFORD & CO., PRINTERS, 9 and 11 WEST FOURTH STREET.

1875.

CONTENTS.

THIRTY-FIRST ANNUAL MEETING

OF THE

Ohio State Medical Society,

HELD AT

PUT-IN-BAY, June 20th, 21st and 22nd, 1876.

FIRST DAY.

MORNING SESSION.

Dr. W. W. Jones, of Toledo, the retiring President, called the meeting to order. Prayer was then had by the Rev. Mr. Bowers.

Dr. Jones thanked the Society for the courtesy and kindness shown him during his term of office, and hoped the members would be as indulgent in their treatment of his successor as they had been with himself. He then presented the President, Dr. E. Williams, who said, he felt deeply the responsibilities of the position to which the Society had elevated him. He said he had been a member of the Society for twenty years, but had not attended regularly the meetings of the Society; and he thought, therefore, some one else should have been chosen President. But since the members had seen proper to select him for the position, he hoped to be able to keep such order as would conduce mostly to the dispatch of business.

2

ADDRESS OF WELCOME.

MR. PRESIDENT,

And Gentlemen of the Ohio State Medical Society:

On behalf of your Executive Committee, the pleasing task is assigned me of greeting you with a hearty welcome. We welcome you to this delightful retreat, where the absence of arduous professional cares and the full, invigorating air bids one breathe deeply,—the expanse of deep, blue waters, with the various picturesque islands, invites the eye and bids us enjoy this panorama of beauty, —this health-laden air, and thus take a new lease of life.

This, the thirty-first annual meeting of this Society, and centennial year of our national existence, would be a fitting time to pass in review the trials and labors the profession have encountered, and the victories that all must have achieved who, like Luke, faithfully and intelligently acted the part of the good physician. But this theme has been so often alluded to that I forbear enlarging on the subject.

Again bidding you a hearty welcome, permit me to express the hope that our meeting may be as profitable as it promises to be pleasant, and that we may return to our life-work with renewed strength and ability to do good.

REPORT OF EXECUTIVE COMMITTEE.

MR. PRESIDENT :

Your Committee beg leave to submit the following report :

The proprietors of this Put-in-Bay House, with their usual liberality, have given us the use of this hall, and such rooms as will be required for committees, free of charge.

The necessary stationery has been provided for the use of the Society.

The rebuffs received from some of the railroad companies, last year, determined your Committee to ask no special favors from them this year. The B. & O., the C. S. & C., D. & M., and perhaps some other roads, will sell excursion round trip tickets, to Put-in-Bay and return, at reduced rates.

ORDER OF BUSINESS.

Your Committee would recommend the same order of business as was adopted last year.

The meeting for daily sessions shall be at 9 A. M. and 2 P. M.

- The order of business for each daily session shall be as follows :

1. Reading of the minutes of the previous session.
- 2. Reports of committee on admissions and election of new members.
3. Reports from officers of the Society.
4. Unfinished business that has not been made a special order.
5. Reports of standing committees.
6. Reports from special committees.
7. Volunteer papers.
8. Miscellaneous business.

The address of the President shall be made a special order for 3 o'clock P. M., Wednesday.

The election of officers shall be made a special order for 2 o'clock P. M., Thursday.

The evenings can be devoted to social re-unions or public lectures,—as may best suit the convenience and inclination of members of the Society.

The legislation of the Society has been so contradictory on the subject of employing a reporter, that your Committee thought best to refer the matter of employing a reporter, or otherwise, to the Society.

All of which is respectfully submitted.

H. J. Donahoe,
Chairman Executive Committee.

REPORT AMENDED.

On motion, the report of the Executive Committee was so amended that the election of officers be had on Wednesday, at 2 o'clock P. M., instead of Thursday, as recommended in the report.

JUDICIAL COUNCIL—INQUIRY.

Dr. A. Dunlap called for the names comprising the Judicial Council, and inquired if the business of the Committee on Ethics was to be transferred to the Judicial Council.

Dr. Hyatt said there was not, as yet, a Judicial Council. The resolution introduced last year to create a Judicial Council, having laid over a year, now comes up for consideration.

Dr. A. Dunlap again inquired, which should act on questions of ethics, the Committee on Ethics or the Judicial Council? This question, he said, should be settled, as there is business of importance to come before the committee at this meeting.

Dr. Jones moved to suspend the rules and adopt the resolution introduced by Dr. Hyatt, last year, amending Section 3rd, Article 3rd, of the By-Laws, abolishing the Committee on Ethics and transferring the duties of that committee to the Judicial Council.

Dr. Ridenour said he thought the Committee on Ethics should finish the business it has on hand, and then the business of that committee might be, for the future, transferred to the Judicial Council.

Dr. Hyatt said he understood the Judicial Council was to take the place of the Committee on Ethics. The resolution introduced, creating the Judicial Council, had laid over one year, and now comes up for consideration.

Dr. Jones then read the resolution transferring the duties of the Committee on Ethics to the Judicial Council, and moved its adoption.

Dr. Hamilton said the Constitution provides for a Committee on Ethics, with certain well defined duties and powers; he could not see the necessity or utility of abolishing that old, well established Committee and substituting something else in its place. He said what he did in the way of caution, for if we go on in this way, abolishing and substituting, we may get our By-laws and our Committees into a jumble.

Dr. Reamy said he thought it strange that we should abolish an old Committee with well defined powers, and substitute something else in its stead.

Dr. Jones said the very name of the Judicial Council implies that it has power to act on all questions that the Committee on Ethics has, and many more questions that the Committee on Ethics has not power to act upon, and questions, too, that often come up in the Society and create a good deal of trouble, and these questions can be settled by the Judicial Council, in a great measure, for its reports are to be confirmed or rejected, without debate.

The question then being, on Dr. Jones' motion, to suspend the rules and adopt Dr. Hyatt's resolution, was put and lost; vote, 13 for, 15 against.

REPORT FROM COMMITTEE ON ADMISSIONS.

The Committee reported the following names for *permanent membership.* Also the following named delegates from auxiliary societies. The question being on the adoption of the report, the motion was put and *carried.*

NEW MEMBERS—Wm. Barker, Attica, O.; Samuel Downs, Waterville, O.; E. M. Webster, Kingsview, Ashtabula Co., O.; J. B. Ford, Norwalk, O.; M. S. Clark, Mahoning Co., O.; Joseph Bington, Williamstown, Va.; E. J. Galbraith, Frankfort, O.; G. S. Franklin, Chillicothe, O.; E. Grissell, Salem, O.; J. H. Pooley, Columbus, O.; C. H. Linskey, Put-in-Bay; J. H. Curry, Toledo, O.; Jerome Bland, Poplar P. O., Crawford Co., O.; J. C. Banning, Round House; B. Tauber, Cincinnati, O.

DELEGATES REPRESENTING AUXILIARY SOCIETIES—C. S. Ward, Franklin Co. Med. Society; J. B. McKechnie, Clinton Med. Society; E. Williams, C. S. Muscroft, T. A. Reamy, J. W. Hadlock, J. H. Buckner, Academy of Med. of Cincinnati; C. A. Kirkly, North-Western Med. Society; S. C. Helmick, Central O. Med. Association; J. H. Curry, Toledo Med. Association; E. Grissell, Union Med. Society; M. S. Clark, Mahoning Co. Med. Society; J. C. Baninger, Washington Co. Med. Society; W. J. Scott, J. Bennett, H. J. Herrick, Cuyahoga Co. Med. Society.

FILLING UP COMMITTEES.

Dr. Hamilton moved that all committees be filled up by appointments of the president to the required number, as some members of committees were absent. Motion put and *carried*.

The President appointed on the Committee on Ethics, W. W. Jones, C. S. Muscroft.

On Finance Committee, J. H. Buckner, Leonard, Thorn.

REPORT FROM COMMITTEE ON MEDICAL SOCIETIES.

Dr. Ridenour, chairman, reported from this Committee in favor of the Ross Co. Medical Society being admitted an Auxiliary Society to the State Society; delegates, E. J. Gilbraith, G. S. Franklin; on motion report *adopted*.

MISCELLANEOUS BUSINESS.

Dr. Ridenour, under this head, called up the amendment proposed last year to Art. VI of the Constitution.

Remarks were made by Drs. Leonard, Gordon and Ridenour on the proposed amendment. The question being on its adoption the motion was put and *lost.*

REPORT OF PUBLICATION COMMITTEE.

Transactions, copies 500	$328 50
Postal card circulars, 630	8 30
Letter heads, 1 ream	6 50
Envelopes 500	2 50
Total	$345 80

J. W. HADLOCK, *Chairman Committee.*

REPORT OF TREASURER AND LIBRARIAN.

TREASURER—Money Collected		$835 25
"	Disbursed	656 33
"	in Treasury	178 92
LIBRARIAN —Copies on hand at beginning of year		1,468
"	Disbursed	696
"	On hand	772

S. S. GRAY, *Treasurer & Librarian.*

On motion, the above reports were *adopted*, except that of the Treasurer, which was referred to the Committee on Finance, for examination and report.

REPORT FROM COMMITTEE ON OBITUARIES.

Dr. Leonard read a report from the above named Committee. In connection with Dr. Leonard's report Dr. Reamy read an obituary of ex-President Dr. Smith, together with a history of the autopsy of Dr. Smith. On motion, these reports were ordered printed with such **ad-ditions** as should be thought proper and necessary.

PARTIAL REPORT FROM COMMITTEE ON FINANCE.

Dr. Hyatt, from this committee, made a partial **report** —in order that members might be paying their dues—**to** the effect that the assessment will be as heretofore, **two** dollars ($2) per annum.   Report *adopted*.

ADVISORY COMMITTEE ON PUBLICATION FILLED UP.

The Advisory Committee on Publication was filled **up** by the appointment of W. W. Jones and J. W. Hamilton on the committee.
Adjourned until 8 o'clock P. M.

————o————

FIRST DAY.

EVENING SESSION.—8 O'CLOCK P. M.

SEMI-INTERNATIONAL MEDICAL SOCIETY.

Dr. Jones reported as follows, in reference to the formation of this society.

MR. PRESIDENT: The committee to confer with similar committees from other States, upon the formation of a Semi-International Medical Society from the States of Ohio, Indiana and Michigan, with the province of Ontario, report, that they have made some progress in calling the attention of the profession of Ontario, with a favorable result, but they have not yet perfected any action.   The Michigan State Medical Society have already promised cordial action. Owing to some inadvertence, the State Medical Society of Indiana have not had the subject presented to them. The Committee therefore report progress, and ask to be continued.

> W. W. JONES,
> A. DUNLAP,
> J. W. HAMILTON,
> E. WILLIAMS,
> JOHN BENNETT,
> *Committee.*

DR. PECK'S CASE.

Dr. A. Dunlap inquired if the charges had been made out against Dr. Peck. The speaker said Dr. Peck had left the State, and he, as Chairman of the Committee on Ethics, had thought it best to drop the case. Remarks were made by a number of the members present, when the matter was, on motion, referred to the Committee on Ethics, with instructions to report.

INQUIRY AND EXPLANATION.

Dr. Gray said two individuals were elected members last year, but their names were not placed with the list of members,—he referred to Drs. Coyle and Larimore. He would like to know why this omission, since they had both paid their dues?

The Secretary stated that, on motion, and by vote of the Society, he was instructed to keep the names of these two gentlemen off the list of members, as there were charges of some irregularity made against them soon after they joined, and which charges were referred to the Committee on Ethics. He had only carried out the instructions of the Society in leaving the names off the list.

DR. W. M. CAKE *vs.* A. S. WILLIAMS, M. D.

Dr. W. M. Cake preferred charges against Dr. A. S. Williams, which charges had previously originated in the

North-western Ohio Medical Association. After some discussion, the matter was referred back to the North-western Ohio Medical Association.

VOLUNTEER PAPERS.

Dr. J. H. Pooley read a paper on " Esmarch's Bandage in Minor Surgery." Referred to Advisory Committee on Publication. [The discussion on this paper will be found published, in connection with the paper.]—SECRETARY.

Dr. Ridenour asked that the Judicial Committee be filled up; which was done by appointing Drs. Bramble, Herrick, Hamilton and Davis on the committee.

Adjourned until 9 A. M., Wednesday.

————o————

SECOND DAY.

————

MORNING SESSION—9 A. M.

Minutes of the previous day read and, after two corrections, adopted.

REPORT FROM FINANCE COMMITTEE.

Dr. Hyatt presented the report from this committee, as follows:

Mr. PRESIDENT: Having examined the account of the Treasurer, together with his papers and vouchers, we find them correct. Whole amount received during the year, $835.25; whole amount disbursed during the year, $656.33; amount in Treasury, 178.92.

PAYMENT OF TREASURER AND SECRETARY.

Your Committee recommend that the Secretary, J. W. Hadlock, be paid, for services, $50; and that S. S. Gray, Treasurer, be paid, for services, $50.

IN REFERENCE TO DELINQUENTS.

Your Committee further recommend that the resolution passed by the Society, three years ago, "dropping from the roll all members after three years' delinquency, and their restoration requiring the payment of all arrears and evidence of proper professional standing given," be sent by the Treasurer to each delinquent, together with a statement of their account.
E. H. HYATT
B. B. LEONARD,
J. H. BUCKNER,
S. S. THORN,
Committee.

On motion, the report was received and *adopted*.

REPORT FROM AMERICAN MEDICAL ASSOCIATION.

Dr. A. Dunlap made a verbal report from the above named Society. There was a full attendance and, taken in all, an interesting meeting. He stated that the President, Dr. Symes, in his address, took the broad ground that the code of Ethics should be abolished, and let every man square his conduct to those principles in usage among gentlemen. He also advocated the admission of Women and Negroes to membership in the American Medical Association. The speaker said, in reference to the International Medical Congress, each State would be entitled to one delegate from each Congressional District.

REPORT FROM MICHIGAN STATE MEDICAL SOCIETY.

Dr. Jones reported from this Society that there was a full meeting, and a very interesting one.

A number of good papers were read and interesting discussions had on them. He said there was a report from the Committee in reference to the question of Homeopathic teachers in the Medical Department of the University of Michigan.   The Committee reported a series of resolutions which gave rise to a debate that was at times acrimonious in character.   Dr. Jones read the resolutions which the Committee reported, and which were adopted by the Michigan State Medical Society.

Dr. Dunlap said this question of these Homeopathic teachers in the University of Michigan had been referred to the Judicial Council of the American Medical Association, to be considered next year.

Dr. Baldwin said that at the late meeting of the American Medical Association, Dr. Toner, of Washington, introduced a motion, which was passed, almost unanimously, to the effect that any practitioneer who would aid or abet the graduation of students in irregular medicine, should be considered as violating the ethics of the American Medical Association; also, that at the convention of Medical Colleges, held just before the meeting of the American Medical Association, a resolution was adopted not to recognize a school in which irregular medicine was taught as a part of its curriculum.   On this subject Dr. J. Bennett introduced the following:

Resolved, That this Society emphatically approves the resolution offered by Dr. Toner, of Washington D. C., and adopted by the American Medical Association at its meeting June 9th, 1876, viz: *Resolved*, that members of the medical profession, who in any way aid or abet the graduation of medical students in irregular or exclusive systems of medicine, are deemed thereby to violate the spirit of the ethics of the American Medical Association.

Dr. Dunlap asked to be excused from voting on the resolutions, as he is a member of the Judicial Council of the American Medical Association, and would be accused of pre-judging the case.   The request was granted.

Dr. Reamy thinks this discussion premature, unprofitable to us and uncalled for, and should be laid aside.   Why should we rush into and discuss a question that does not concern our Society in the least? Why take up the time of the Society with the discussion of this quarrel that alone concerns the Michigan State Society and Michigan University, to the exclusion of other and more profitable business? Dr. Dunlap comes here from the American Medical Association, and reports a quarrel and fight from that quarter. Dr. Jones comes freighted with the report of a big quarrel from the Michigan State Medical Society—neither one of these gentlemen come laden with glad tidings of things said or done for the healing and relief of suffering humanity—neither comes with healing on his wings and with the joyful news of "on earth peace, good will to man"; no, nothing but quarrels and dissensions; and are we expected to take up the echo of these discordant sounds and hand them along the line and leave our own business half or entirely undone? Let us drop these unprofitable discussions and have none of them.

Dr. Herrick moved to lay the resolutions on the table. *Carried.*

REPORT FROM COMMITTEE ON ADMISSIONS.

The Committee on admissions reported in favor of the following names for permanent members; also the following delegates from auxiliary societies. On motion the report was *adopted:*

NEW MEMBERS—F. S. Helbish, Green Springs, O.; A. E. Merrill, Vermillion; J. B. McKechnie, Wilmington, O.; S. H. Brown, Dennison; J. Campbell, Dennison; D. M. Vance, Urbana; J. H. Ayers, Urbana; James Smith, Clarington; W. S. Fisher, Bridgeport.

DELEGATES—John M. Welsh, Stillwater Medical Society; J. D. Edwards, Greene Co. Medical Society; W. S.

Fisher, M. W. Junkins, Medico-Chirurgical Society, Eastern O.; Drs. Speer, Larimore, Gamion and Rogers, Licking Co. Medical Society.

COMMITTEE ON MEDICAL SOCIETIES' REPORT.

Dr. Ridenour, from this Committee, reported in favor of the Medico-Chirurgical Society of North-Eastern Ohio being admitted as an auxiliary society. The report said that the Licking County Medical Society had purged itself of the charges made against it last year, and still remains an auxiliary society. On motion the report was *adopted*.

Dr. Dunlap moved that the name of Dr. Larimore be placed on the list of membership. *Carried.*

VOLUNTEER PAPER—NEW FORCEPS.

Dr. A. J. Miles read a volunteer paper descriptive of a new forceps and explaining its utility in breech presentations. The instrument was invented by himself.

Pending the reference of this paper a discussion embracing a wide field, was indulged in on instruments, in general, as employed in obstetric practice. Some, and the majority present, advocated their timely and judicious use, whilst a few said they had discarded them quite or altogether.

Dr. Reamy made a forcible speech in favor of the judicious use of instruments in the obstetric art, and said for the first eight years of his practice through such teaching as he had heard here to-day he was induced to not use them at all, and the result was that he could now look back and reproach himself that he had lost cases that the timely use of instruments might have saved. In extreme cases he not only considered it proper to resort to the use of instruments, but he held it to be the bounden and absolute *duty* of the obstetrician to resort to their use. It is too late in the day to cry out against the use of instruments when we see weekly good results flow from their use, in many cases, that would otherwise prove fatal.

Dr. C. E. Beardsley introduced the following, which was *carried unanimously*:

WHEREAS, Dr. L. W. Moe, a veteran in the medical profession, also an esteemed and honorable member of this Society from its organization, and prior to its formation, was a faithful member of the old State Medical Convention, and,

WHEREAS, Dr. Moe, from the effect of disease, has become totally and hopelessly blind, therefore,

Resolved, That this Society extend to him its sympathies, and to show our appreciation of his moral excellence, by unanimously electing him a permanent member of this Association ; thus relieving him from further financial obligations as a member. Recess until 2 P. M.

————O————

SECOND DAY.

AFTERNOON SESSION.

REPORT FROM COMMITTEE ON ETHICS.

Dr. A. Dunlap, from this committee, reported as follows :

As Dr. Coyle is not present, this Committee recommends the continuance of his case for one year. Upon the statement made by Drs. Reed and Kelley of the facts, we release them from blame resulting from their recommendation of Dr. Coyle. Report *adopted.*

ELECTION OF OFFICERS.

The election of officers for the ensuing year resulted as follows:

W. J. Scott, Cleveland, *President.*
T. W. Gordon, Georgetown, ⎫
A. J. Miles, Cincinnati, ⎪
J. G. Nolen, Toledo, ⎬ *Vice-Presidents.*
W. T. Ridenour, Toledo, ⎭
S. S. Gray, Piqua, *Treasurer.*
J. W. Hadlock, Cincinnati, *Secretary.*
J. F. Baldwin, Columbus, *Assistant Secretary.*
C. E. Beardsley, Ottawa, ⎫
H. C. Pierce, Urbana, ⎪
C. Dunlap, Springfield, ⎬ *Com. on Admissions.*
M. W. Junkins, Bellair, ⎪
J. Bennett, Cleveland, ⎭

REPORT FROM JUDICIAL COUNCIL—PLACE OF MEETING.

Dr. Ridenour, from this committee, reported in favor of meeting at Put-in-Bay, in 1877, on the second Tuesday in June, at 2 o'clock P. M., as the proprietors of the Put-in-Bay House had agreed to entertain the members and their families at $2.00 per day each, if the meeting takes place anywhere between the 19th of May and the 20th of June.

On motion, the report was *adopted.*

REPORT FROM THE SANITARY COMMITTEE.

Dr. E. H. Hyatt, Chairman of this committee, said:

Mr. President: The Sanitary Committee, consisting of one member from each Congressional District, to whom was referred, last year, the matter of memorializing the Legislature for the creation, by law, of a State Sanitary Commission, submit the following brief report:

A bill was drafted by your Committee creating a Sanitary Board, with power to elect a Superintendent of Vital Statistics, at a salary of $3,000 per annum; and said bill was presented by the Member of the House from Delaware, Dr. J. A. Carothers, and read, but failed to pass because the Legislature did not wish, at that time, to create any new salaried offices.

Your Committee have hope, from the favor it received last winter, that said bill will yet receive the sanction of the Legislature.

INFORMATION WANTED.

The Ross County Medical Society asked for instructions, and were referred to the Judicial Council, which was instructed to report at this meeting. Report further on.

VOLUNTEER PAPERS.

Dr. B. Tauber read a paper on Stenosis of the Larynx.

Dr. W. H. Mussey read a short paper on "Tumours Aurien," so-called, following the reduction of a subglenoid dislocation of the head of the humerus.

Dr. A. N. Reed read a short paper on the "External use of Glycerine for the cure of Chronic Hydrocephalus."

Dr. Reamy, from special committee on Gynaecology, reported seven cases of cancer of the cervix uteri, in which he had removed the neck, giving the results. This paper gave rise to an animated and interesting discussion, which will be found published in connection with the paper.

On motion, adjourned until 8 o'clock P. M.

3

SECOND DAY.

EVENING SESSION.

NATIONAL MEDICAL LIBRARY.

Dr. J. B. Bennett introduced the following:

Resolved, That the President of this Society appoint a committee of twenty-one, to memorialize Congress with reference to the catalogue of the National Medical Library, and respectfully urge such appropriation as will secure the early completion of the work already begun by the Surgeon-General.

On motion, the resolution was so amended that the committee of twenty-one be taken one from each Congressional District, and each member of the committee to confer with the Congressman of his District.

The resolution was then laid on the table.

PRESIDENT'S ADDRESS: " PENETRATING WOUNDS OF THE EYE."

Dr. Leonard was called to the Chair while the President read his address; the subject being, "Penetrating wounds of the Eye."

Dr. Hyatt thought the paper too valuable to be buried in the transactions; it ought to go to the profession at large.

In reply to a question by Dr. Pooly, Dr. Williams said, that a cloudiness, referred to by the patient, to the side opposite of the point where the foreign body rests, is of value as a diagnostic point.

Dr. Pooly then stated a case of this nature.

Paper referred to Advisory Committee on Publication.

CONGRATULATIONS.

Dr. Jones moved the following:

To the President of the New York State Medical Society, Albany, N. Y. :

The Ohio State Medical Society convened at Put-in-Bay, June 21st, 1876, greet your Society in endeavors to promote progress in medicine.

Carried.

To this the following was received:

ALBANY, N. Y., June 22, 1876.

E. Williams, Pres't State Med. Society of Ohio, Put-in-Bay.

The Medical Society of the State of New York will co-operate most cordially. Push on the good work.

THOS. F. ROCHESTER, *Pres't.*

RESOLUTION TO MEMORIALIZE CONGRESS TAKEN FROM THE TABLE.

· Dr. Reamy moved that the resolution of Dr. Bennett be taken from the table and passed as amended. The motion prevailed, and the resolution passed accordingly.

THIRD DAY.

Minutes of the previous day read, and after a few corrections, were *adopted*.

ETHICAL RESOLUTIONS TO PURGE, PURIFY AND CLEANSE.

Dr. Mussey introduced the following:

WHEREAS, At a meeting of the Judicial Council it was made known that the Academy of Medicine of Columbus, Ohio, retains within its limits one or more members who defiantly consult with irregular practitioneers, and that the members of the Society are fully cognizant of these irregularities, and have taken no measures to purge the Society of the member or members referred to, therefore,

Resolved, That this Society directs the Academy of Medicine of Columbus, to investigate the statement, and, if found to be true, to discipline any such members, and purge the Society from this disgrace, and report to the Society at the next annual meeting.

To this Dr. J. H. Pooley offered the following amendment, which was accepted by Dr. Mussey:

Resolved, also, That this Society disapproves of admitting the reporters of the secular daily press to the meetings of a Medical Society, as is done in the Columbus Academy of Medicine.

Resolved, also, That this Society disapproves of the practice of regular physicians advertising themselves as specialists in medicine, in the secular press, and think that such societies as the Columbus Academy of Medicine should not allow such action on the part of its members.

The introduction of these resolutions was the signal for war, and gave rise to a warm discussion, becoming, at times, almost personal in character; still, Dr. Mussey bore himself well throughout the entire engagement. Even after the battle became general, he seemed calm and serene amid the storm he had raised, and above the din and roar of battle he was heard to exclaim, ''REFORM is the word, this is the centennial year of *reform*; the two great political parties have bespangled their philacteries with the word, and ere this stammering tongue is gathered to the fathers I hope to see it emblazoned on the banner of medicine, and every doctor stand out as fair as the moon, as bright as the sun and as terrible as—I am to all irregulars and •irregularities in our noble, humane and self-sacrificing profession." Motions rained thick and fast—to dismiss, to lay on the table, to lay over, etc., etc., etc.

The question of admitting reporters of the secular press to local medical societies for the purpose of reporting the proceedings and puffing favorites; of advertising cases— especially surgical cases; of advertising clinics with the mention of the clinician, was all passed in review—each and every speaker having his word of good advice, as well as admonition to evil doers. Finally a motion to lay on the table prevailed.

Dr. Davis then introduced the following, which, on motion, was referred to the Judicial Committee:

WHEREAS, It is currently reported that Mrs. P. B. Sauer, of Napoleon, Ohio, a member of the State Medical Society of Ohio, and a member of the N. W. Medical Society, is now practicing so called homeopathy, therefore be it

Resolved, That the North-western Medical Association be instructed to examine and report as to the truth of the allegation.   '   W. B. DAVIS.

Dr. Pooley then presented the following two resolutions:

Resolved, That advertising by members of this Society and its auxiliaries, in public journals, or by circulars or handbills, of free clinics for the poor, with the names of the clinicians, is irregular and in violation of the code of ethics.

Resolved, That the Ohio State Medical Society hereby directs all its auxiliary societies to prohibit the printing of medical cases or the proceedings of such auxiliary societies, in the secular newspapers, and especially the naming of physicians in connection therewith.

Dr. Hyatt to the last resolution offered the following amendment:

Resolved, That the State Society be included in the foregoing resolution.

After some further discussion, Dr. Mussey presented his resolutions anew, when the whole matter was, on motion, referred to the Judicial Council.

Dr. W. B. Davis introduced the following:

Resolved, That graduates of irregular medical colleges, or physicians who have practiced irregularly, or been guilty of quackery, shall not be elegible to membership in the State Society until they have publicly repudiated their irregular practice, and graduated from a regular medical college. *Carried.*

CONCERNING DR. BUCKNER'S PAPER ON ASTIGMATISM.

Dr. Muscroft read the following:

WHEREAS, The published minutes of this Society in the proceedings of last year, in reference to the ˙paper of Dr. Buckner upon Astigmatism, are incomplete, in so much as they do not give the discussion of it, and fail, also, to state that the Advisory Committee reconsidered their action, and requested that the paper be made shorter by leaving off the historical part, and be handed to a member of the Committee for publication; thereby making a record which does injustice to its author.

Resolved, That it is the opinion of this Society that the paper of Dr. Buckner upon astigmatism, read at its meeting last June, treated in an able manner a scientific subject of interest to the medical profession, and of great importance to eye specialists.

Resolved, That the reconsidered action of the Advisory Committee as expressed in favor of the publication of an abstract of said paper meets with the endorsement of this Society.

Resolved, That these resolutions be published in the proceedings of this body for this year.

After an explanation by Dr. Buckner and the secretary, the above resolutions were *adopted unanimously*.

Dr. Ridenour introduced the following:

Resolved, That all candidates for admission to the Ohio State Medical Society be requested to present their diplomas and certificates of standing and character to the Committee on Admissions. *Carried.*

REPORT FROM THE JUDICIAL COUNCIL.

Dr. Ridenour presented the following from the Judicial Council, which was adopted :

Statement of Facts, and Request for Instructions from the Ross County Medical Society.

There are two medical societies in Ross County, Ohio—the Chillicothe Academy of Medicine, and the Ross County Medical Society. The first of these ignores the code of ethics. It contains in its membership some regular medical men who, themselves, try to obey the code, still giving their countenance and support to other men who notoriously practice quackery and refuse to obey the code. Some of those men who are willing to obey the code wish to join the Ross County Medical Society (now an auxiliary to the State Medical Society), *and at the same time they wish to belong to the other society.* The Ross County Medical Society, through its delegates, here present, wish to be instructed as to the following points:

1. Can a medical man belong properly to both societies?
2. Ought the members of the Ross County Medical Society to consult with members of the Chillicothe Academy of Medicine, as long as that society avowedly ignores the code of ethics?

Respectfully submitted to the State Medical Society.

E. J. GALBRAITH, M. D.
G. S. FRANKLIN, M. D.
Delegates from Ross County.

The within request for instructions presented by delegates from the Ross County Medical Society, was referred to the Judicial Council of the Ohio State Medical Society for immediate answer.

To the questions given, the answer is as follows:

Question 1—Can a medical man properly belong to both societies?

Answer—He cannot.

Question 2—Is it right for the members of the Ross County Medical Society to consult with members of the Chillicothe Academy of Medicine *as long as that society avowedly ignores the code of ethics?*

Answer—It is the opinion of the Judicial Council that no member of a society auxiliary to the State Medical Society can hold professional relations with the members of a society that repudiates the code of ethics and consorts with quacks and irregulars.

[Signed by the Judicial Council.]

VOLUNTEER PAPERS CONTINUED.

Dr. Muscroft read a paper on Foreign Bodies in the Rectum. Discussion on the paper postponed, and paper referred to Advisory Committee.

Dr. Davis stated that he had intended preparing a paper on Jennerian and Cowpox Vaccination, and also on Syphilitic Vaccinia. He had corresponded with the leading men in Europe who had given this subject especial attention, but he had not heard from all of them in time to prepare his paper. He had, however, a number of the letters received with him, and would read them if the society wished. He then read the letters referred to.

Dr. Jones moved that Dr. Davis be requested to prepare his paper and have it published in the transactions this year, together with the letters he had just read. *Carried.*

It was moved that the Secretary inform the gentlemen whose letters had just been read, that their letters had been received and read, and that they had been elected honorary and corresponding members of this society. *Carried.*

Dr. Davis then read a paper, prepared by Dr. E. B. Stevens, on The Hot Springs of Arkansas. Paper referred to Advisory Committee.

ETHICAL AUTHORITY TRANSFERRED TO JUDICIAL COUNCIL.

Dr. Jones moved to adopt Dr. Hyatt's resolution, on page 25 of the published minutes of last year, transferring the business of the Committee on Ethics to the Judicial Council. *Carried.*

REPORT OF THE ADVISORY COMMITTEE ON PUBLICATION.

Dr. Ridenour made the following report from the above named committee:

The Advisory Committee recommend the publication of all papers read at this meeting, together with as full a report as possible of the discussions thereon. This includes the papers of Drs. Muscroft and Davis, and the paper or letter of Dr. Stevens, as read by Dr. Davis.

J. BENNETT,
W. T. RIDENOUR,
W. H. MUSSEY,
SAM'L S. THORN,
Committee.

THE JUDICIAL COUNCIL—CORRECTION.

The following is the true copy of the resolution, as amended, creating the Judicial Council, the rough draft having been, by mistake, previously substituted:

Resolved, That a Judicial Council of seven be appointed annually by the President, to whom shall be referred all business of a legislative character, including time and place of meeting; and their report shall be confirmed, or rejected, without debate by the society.

W. T. RIDENOUR.

AUXILIARY SOCIETIES—LIST CALLED FOR.

Dr. Ridenour introduced the following resolution, which was adopted:

Resolved, That the Secretary and Committee on Publication be instructed to include in the volume of transactions for this year, a list of the auxiliary societies to this society.

[In accordance with the above resolution, we have endeavored to furnish a complete list of the auxiliary societies to the State Society; but we have reason to fear that it is not a full list, as we found it impossible to procure a complete set of the transactions, from which to make the list. Those knowing of other societies than those named, being auxiliary, will confer a favor by reporting the 'same to the Secretary, or to the next meeting of the State Society. J. W. H.]

Shelby County Medical Society.
Champaign County Medical Society.
Darke County Medical Society.
Pickaway County Medical Society.
Green County Medical Society.
Toledo Medical Association.
Medina County Medical Society.
Delamater Medical Association of Norwalk.
Jefferson County Medical Society.
Allen County Medical Society.
Trumbull County Medical Society.
Clermont County Medical Society.
Montgomery County Medical Society.
Meigs County Medical Society.
Scioto County Medical Society.
Butler County Medical Society.
Portage County Medical Society.
Central Ohio Medical Association (Westerville).
Holmes County Medical Society.
North-western Ohio Medical Association.
Fulton County Medical Society.
Academy of Medicine of Cincinnati.
Cincinnati Medical Society.
Ross County Medical Society.
Medico-Chirurgical Society of N. E. Ohio.
Licking County Medical Society.

Franklin County Medical Society.
Clinton County Medical Society.
Union Medical Association.
Mahoning County Medical Society.
Washington County Medical Society.
Cuyahoga County Medical Society.
Stillwater Medical Society.
Columbus Academy of Medicine.

————o————

COMMITTEES.—STANDING AND SPECIAL.

STANDING COMMITTEES.

Advisory Committee on Publication.

CLEVELAND.

H. J. Herrick,
John Bennett,
W. J. Scott.

CINCINNATI.

W. H. Mussey,
T. A. Reamy,
D. D. Bramble.

TOLEDO.

W. W. Jones,
J. M. Haddick,
S. S. Thorn.

COLUMBUS.

J. W. Hamilton,
E. H. Hyatt,
A. Dunlap.

Committee on Publication.

W. B. Davis,
J. W. Hadlock,
C. S. Muscroft,
P. S. Conner.
} Cincinnati.

Committee on Medical Societies.

S. S. Thorn,
A. C. McLaughlin,

H. J. Herrick,
Jonathan Norris.

Executive Committee.

H. J. Donahoe, Sandusky, Chairman.
C. H. Kirkley, Toledo.
C. M. Dunlap, Springfield.
John Bennett, Cleveland.
C. H. J. Linskey, Put-in-Bay.

Committee on Obituaries.

B. B. Leonard, West Liberty.

Committee to Memorialize Congress on Catalogue.

1—W. W. Dawson, Cincinnati.
2—M. B. Wright,   "
3—N. H. Sidwell, Wilmington.
4—Clark McDermout, Dayton.
5—C. E. Beardsley, Ottawa.
6—W. W. Jones, Toledo.
7—G. S. Franklin, Chillicothe.
8—H. W. Phillips, Kenton.
9—T. B. Williams, Delaware.
10—E. Stanley, Sandusky.
11—W. F. Wilson, Ironton.
12—Jesse Thompson, Bloomfield.
13—Howard Culbertson, Zanesville.
14—Benj. Myers, Ashland.
15—Richard Gundry, Athens.
16—W. S. Fisher, Bridgeport.
17—T. Woodbridge, Youngstown.
18—J. D. Robinson, Wooster.
19—D. B. Wood, Warren.
20—J. C. E. Weber, Cleveland.

Committee on Semi-International Medical Society.

W. W. Jones,   John Bennett,
J. W. Hamilton,   A. Dunlap,
      E. Williams.

Judicial Council.

W. T. Ridenour,   W. H. Mussey,
A. T. Keyt,   John Bennett,
J. H. Pooley,   W. J. Conklin,
     Thos. G. McE'Bright.

Committee on Finance.

E. J. McCollum,   C. E. Beardsley,
C. N. Read,   T. G. McE'Bright,
     Sam'l D. Lumey.

Committee to Memorialize the Legislature in favor of an Asylum for Inebriates.

J. W. Russell.   E. W. Howard.

SPECIAL COMMITTEES.

E. H. Hyatt, Pathology of Albuminuria.

T. A. Reamy, Gynaecology.

P. S. Conner, Syphilis in its Hygienic relations.

J. H. Buckner, Influence of Affections of the Throat on the Eye.

J. R. Black, Atmospheric and Telluric influence in Etiology.

S. S. Gray, Milk Sickness.

I. H. Curry, On Eye.

A. J. Miles, Forceps in Breech Delivery.

J. Bennett, Malaria.

Thos. W. Gordon, Quinine in Controlling Fever Heat.

B. Tauber, Diseases of the Larynx and Air Passages.

J. B. Hough, Spontaneous Generation—Nature of the Evidences of.

Wm. Clendenin, The Influence of Drainage on the Public Health.

DELEGATES TO THE INTERNATIONAL MEDICAL CONGRESS.

W. J. Scott, Cleveland; W. W. Jones, (S. S. Thorn, Alternate,) Toledo; W. H. Mussey, Cincinnati; Wm. Carson, Cincinnati; A. N. Reed, Norwalk; H. J. Herrick, Cleveland; T. W. Gordon, Georgetown; L. Firestone, Wooster; A. Hurd, Findlay; W. D. Scarf, Bellfontaine; J. H. Pooley, Columbus; J. W. Hamilton, Columbus; Enoch Pearce, Steubenville; Howard Culbertson, Zanesville; Cyrus Falconer, Hamilton; J. C. Hubbard, Ashtabula; B. F. Hart, Marietta; W. J. McDowell, Portsmouth; C. E. Beardsley, Ottawa; J. C. Reeve, Dayton; Geo. Mitchel, Mansfield; E. Williams, Cincinnati; R. Bartholow, Cincinnati; G. C. E. Weber, Cleveland.

Delegates at Large.

W. B. Davis, J. W. Hadlock, Cincinnati.

DELEGATES TO THE AMERICAN MEDICAL ASSOCIATION.

S. F. Forbes, Toledo; C. A. Kirkley, Toledo; A. N. Reed, Norwalk; W. C. Chapman, Toledo; J. Priest, Toledo; T. W. Gordon, Georgetown; H. J. Donohoe, Sandusky; E. J. McCollum, Tiffin; C. M. McConnelly, Vermillion; A. Dunlop, Springfield; W. J. Scott, Cleveland; J. M. Waddick, Toledo; T. C. Miller, Massillon; J. Larimore, Newark; E. H. Hyatt, Delaware; E. Williams, Cincinnati; J. W. Hadlock, Cincinnati; S. S. Thorn, Toledo; W. T. Ridenour, Toledo; W. W. Jones, Toledo; A. J. Gawn, Cleveland; John Bennett, Cleveland; B. W. Halliday, Cleveland; J. N. Stockwell, New Carlisle; J. W. Hamilton, Columbus; N. Gay, J. F. Baldwin, R. M. Dennig, S. Loving, Columbus; M. S. Mead, Cleveland; E. B. Pratt, Mt. Sterling; Jesse Thompson, Bloomfield; J. D. Robinson, Wooster; J. M. Weaver, Soldiers' Home; F. J. Weed, Cleveland; J. H. Pooley, Columbus; S. S. Gray, Piqua; W. C. Chapman, Toledo; B. F. Hart, Marietta; Philo E. Jones, Wauseon; H. A. Root, Toledo; M. W. Jenkins, Bellaire; J. M. Crafts, Mantua; A. J. Miles, Cincinnati.

DELEGATES TO STATE MEDICAL SOCIETIES.

Michigan—W. W. Jones, J. W. Hamilton, R. C. S. Reed, W. W. Dawson.

Indiana—A. Dunlap, T. A. Reamy, W. H. Mussey, S. S. Thorn.

Kentucky—T. W. Gordon, A. J. Miles, J. F. Baldwin, J. W. Hadlock.

West Virginia—A. B. Jones, C. M. Finch, James Moore, W. P. Kincaid.

New York—R. Bartholow, J. A. Murphy, J. R. Black, J. H. Pooley, C. G. Comegys, R. R. McIlvaine.

The meeting adjourned to meet at Put-in-Bay the second Tuesday in June, 1877.

E. WILLIAMS, M. D., President.

J. W. HADLOCK, M. D., Secretary.

J. F. BALDWIN, M. D., Assistant Secretary.

[The meeting just closed will long be remembered by all present as the one of good feeling. Good papers, good speeches characterized the proceedings throughout. Our entertainers did all in their power to make our stay pleasant, and they succeeded in an eminent degree. With the good sailing, good rowing, good fishing, and good fun generally, the meeting of the State Society in the Centennial year will long be remembered.   J. W. H.]

MINUTES OF THE PUBLICATION COMMITTEE.

CINCINNATI, July 15th, 1876.

At the call of the Chairman, the above committee met at the office of Dr. W. B. Davis.

Dr. Hadlock acted as Secretary, and Dr. Davis presided.

Bids, to print the transactions, from the following houses, were opened and read, the bids having been made on the basis of 550 copies of 175 pages each, and to be equal in all respects to the transactions of 1875 :

Wilstach, Baldwin & Co., $412 50; Methodist Book Concern, $345 17; Miami Helmet Office, Piqua, O., $275; Gazette Publishing Co., $270 50; A. H. Pounsford & Co., $250.

Dr. Muscroft moved that the job be given to A. H. Pounsford & Co., as their bid was the lowest made, and also that the Treasurer of the State Society be instructed to place the amount on deposit in Cincinnati on or before the 15th day of August, 1876, subject to the order of Dr. W. B. Davis. *Carried.*

Dr. Muscroft moved that the Secretary furnish a copy of the proceedings of this meeting to the Treasurer of the State Society, and furnish a copy for publication in the transactions for 1876. *Carried.*

Dr. Hadlock moved that each author be requested to read the proof of his own paper, copies to be furnished him by the publisher. *Carried.*

Meeting adjourned.

W. B. DAVIS, Chairman.

J. W. HADLOCK, Secretary.

ANNUAL ADDRESS

——OF THE——

RETIRING PRESIDENT, E. WILLIAMS, M. D.,

CINCINNATI, OHIO.

ANNUAL ADDRESS

— OF THE —

RETIRING PRESIDENT, E. WILLIAMS, M. D.,

CINCINNATI, O.

GENTLEMEN :—The third object, in order, of this association, is "the cultivation and advancement of medical science and literature, and the elevation of the standard of professional education." The best way to advance knowledge and elevate the professional standard, is to improve and reform ourselves by earnest and hearty work, so that our neighbors, seeing our good works, may glorify us and not we ourselves. Let each member remove the beam from his own eye, subdue his own hard heart and store his brain with well-ordered and useful knowledge, and he is certain to esteem others better than himself, and not likely to be the first to sling projectiles among his neighbors, be they ever so ignorant or ever so wayward. In this spirit, I shall not begin with an eulogy of the great, regular profession, much less with a philippic against its lilliputian rivals and adversaries. I appreciate the honarable position you have conferred upon me, and will not abuse it by flattering you or charging upon the poor *Isms and Pathies*. I cannot even compliment you upon the wisdom of your executive choice. So the less said about it, the more creditable both to you and myself. It is a wise maxim seldom felt in its full force, that the longer we live the less time we have. So let us work while it is day.

I propose to occupy your attention for a short time with
a practical and very important subject:

PENETRATING WOUNDS OF THE EYE.

This precious little organ may be injured in many ways,
and by a vast variety of objects.   A point of prime importance is whether the offending body has entered the
eye ball.   To determine this, is by no means easy in very
many cases.   If the wound is large and deep, the immediate partial or complete collapse of the globe and the
escape of a part of its peculiar contents, reveal at once to
the most ignorant or even careless, the nature of the injury.
But if the injuring body is small and propelled with great
force, it may penetrate deep into the eye with a scarcely
perceptible wound and almost without pain.   The patient
himself *knows* it could not have gone into his eye, for he *hardly felt it*, and he often misleads his physician.   It is well known
to surgeons of experience that a small particle flying with
great force and lodging deep in the eye, hurts much less than
when moving slowly and lodging on the eye, or under the
lid.   Besides the pain is much greater for hours and even
days and weeks afterwards, in the latter case than in the
former.   It frequently happens that a foreign body of minute size penetrates the eye, producing sooner or later
cataract or other serious trouble, and the patient cannot
remember when, where or how it could have occurred, so
little did it attract his attention at the fatal moment.   This
should warn us to make a most minute and critical examination of every eye where the circumstances prove such
an occurrence possible.   For instance a slight sting is felt
in the eye of a bystander, when a percussion cap is exploded.   He rubs the eye for a moment, wipes away a
tear, and feels it no more.   On close inspection a particle
of the cylinder has passed through the cornea and lodged
in the anterior chamber, the iris, the lens, or even cleared

all of these and gone deep into the vitreous, causing perhaps very little immediate impairment of vision. The first step in the diagnosis is to find the wound. The second, to determine whether it extends through all the coats of the eye. And thirdly, has the injuring body rebounded, lodged in the tunics themselves or cleared them and entered the globe to remain. In seeking the wound each part of the ball must be inspected in systematic order, beginning with the one most commonly injured, the cornea. In the examination we may be guided often, with some certainty, to the seat of the injury, by the circumstances under which it occurred, and the existence of a scratch or a cut of one or the other eye-lid. As the eye is nearly always open at such times, if the body is small it strikes the cornea directly, without grazing or passing through the lids. It is in these cases where oft times the diagnosis is extremely difficult. The cornea, covered by its smooth, polished epithelium, acts as a reflector forming images of objects in front of it. If the epithelium at any point is abraded or rough, a corresponding blur and defect will be seen in the sharp image of the window towards which it looks. The eye should be examined at an angle and made to move slowly that the little image may travel over its whole surface in succession. Another excellent means of detecting a very small scratch or wound in the cornea is by oblique illumination. Darken the room and light your gas or lamp, seat your patient facing it and concentrate the light upon the cornea by a strong convex lens of 2 or 3 inches focus. If an abrasion or wound, be it ever so minute, exists, you will thus see it. Of course if the cut is large, with hernia of the iris, it is seen at once without these valuable aids.

Discovered the seat of the wound, has it penetrated? If the iris is drawn into it by the escape of aqueous humor, forming a hernia, ever so small, *yes.* If the chamber has its relations altered, that is, if the iris is near or in contact

with the cornea, whether prolapsed or not, *yes*.   If there is
blood in the chamber, much or little, without the possibility of a severe concussion of the eye, with or without
unnatural softness of the ball to the touch, *yes*.   If a small
hole is seen in the iris corresponding in size to the corneal
wound and in the probable direction of the penetrating
body, with or without blood in the chamber or alteration
of the depth of the chamber, *yes*.   If the foreign body can
be certainly seen in the iris, lens or chamber, *yes*.   If, with
the wound of the cornea, with or without changes in the
chamber or the tension of the globe, the lens is becoming
certainly milky, showing beginning cataract, with perhaps
a visible wound in its capsule, *yes*.   All of these symptoms
failing, in a case of manifest wound of the cornea, you
dilate the pupil and use the ophthalmoscope.   If the fundus
of the eye is darkened by blood, the circumstances pre-
cluding rupture of intraocular vessels, there is almost certainly penetration.   If the foreign body can be positively
seen within the organ, in the chamber, iris, lens, vitreous,
or retina, the diagnosis is sure.   Of course impairment of
sight and the appearance of a cloud in the field of vision,
caused by extravasated blood or the foreign body, or both,
come in as corroborative evidence of penetration.   The
sight may be destroyed at once or very soon; or it may
be little effected, according to the size, direction and final
resting place of the offending body.   The value of softness
of the globe, as an evidence of penetration, is very great,
when it certainly is present.   But the tension is often not
altered.   If the foreign body is small, it may pass deep
into the eye wihout any escape of humor, either aqueous
or vitreous, and hence leave the tension normal.

When the patient is not seen for some minutes, hours,
or even days after the injury, the wound may be firmly
closed and the lost humors reproduced, so that undue softness is no longer present.   The reproduction of lost
humors is very rapid, as is known to all operators on the

eye. In fact, if the patient is not seen for several days, the eye may be too hard, from internal inflammation and secretion ; this *increased tension* then becoming the indirect evidence of penetration.

The ophthalmoscopic evidence of penetration, when positive, that is, when the body itself is seen, or suffused blood, or a cloudy sleeve of opacity along its track in the vitreous, is quite sufficient. Still, the result of such an examination may be altogether negative, and yet the offender be in the eye. Should it rest far forward in the vitreous—behind the iris or ciliary circle—it is detected with great difficulty, if at all. In that case, there being none of the symptoms already emphasized, we should make a reserved diagnosis and wait for further developments. Should the extraneous body be in the eye, it is almost certain to give rise to trouble sooner or later. Moreover, the supposed visible intruder may prove to be a globule of blood, or air, or both; but that does not invalidate its importance as an evidence of penetration. On the question of the presence actually in the eye, of the foreign body, it may leave doubt which can only be cleared up by time. So the cloud seen by the patient, after an injury, may or may not be caused by the presence of a foreign body in the globe, but is a strong presumptive proof of penetration. So much for foreign bodies entering through the cornea without regard to their continued presence in the eye.

But the eye may be struck behind the cornea, in the sclerotic region. And as this part of the globe is covered by conjunctiva and capsule of tenon,—both thin, elastic and movable on its surface,—the wound may easily escape notice when small. Its torn edges, and especially the ecchymosis always present, perhaps, for a short time after the injury, will attract attention to the injured spot. The thing, then, has struck there, but has it entered? If the spot is over the sclero-corneal junction, or very little back of it, we may still look in the anterior chamber for signs of the passage of the wounding body. The iris may be wounded near its ciliary margin, or a small knuckle of its periphery protruding through the wound. Blood in the aqueous chamber has here also the same positive significance. Should neither prolapsus iridis, hemorrhage, nor any appreciable rent in the iris be discovered, it is still wise to make a scrutinizing search with the ophthalmoscope, in this, as in all cases of suspicious injuries of the eye-ball. Physicians in general pass too lightly over such accidents, assuring the patient at once, perhaps, that nothing is in the eye.

I would insist upon the importance of small wounds of the iris, sometimes forming a sharp hole in this curtain, admitting light and giving a red reflex from the bottom of the eye with the ophthalmoscope. They prove not only penetration, but the almost infallible presence of the foreign body in the back of the eye. A very small hole or cut in the iris, can only be made by the passage of a very small body, and one which must clear the cornea before striking the iris. Rebounding in that case is impossible. Such an injury could only be the result of a small body, or a pin or needle, splinter, or some long, slender projectile. In the latter instance, the thing might rebound. In case it has also cleared the iris and is hence invisible, it may be found in the suspensory ligament or margin of the lens, or in the vitreous behind it. The body being small and the edge of the lens barely grazed, there is not likely to be traumatic cataract, an *infallibe evidence* of penetration when *it is detected*. The ophthalmoscope may or may not detect it in the fundus. The same observations made above about ophthalmoscopic evidences of penetration and their significance, apply here.

If the wound in the conjunctiva and sclerotic is large, and made either by a large body entering directly or glancing, there will probably be loss of vitreous, with its characteristic ropiness, and flabbiness or collapse of the globe. In this event, the foreign body may be lodged in the globe or not. In such destructive injuries there is almost certainly free hemorrhage within the eye, preventing any immediate inspection of the fundus. But a wound of the sclerotic conjunctiva does not necessarily indicate penetration. The injuring body may have glanced backwards between the conjunctiva and sclerotic piercing the latter perhaps in the region of the equator, or sparing the globe and plunging deep into the socket. Sometimes a shot, or scale of metal, when driven with great force, passes entirely through the globe and lodges in the apex of the orbit. In rare cases a rough scale may be found grasped by the sclerotic after having traversed the vitreous.

Some years ago a machinist called on me with an injured eye. There was a large ragged wound in the sclerotic, the ball flabby and filled with blood. I was sure that a rough scale of metal had entered deeply and remained in the ball. Immediate enucleation was urged, but he would not consent. The eye was hopelessly lost; great suffering would ensue, involving much danger to the other eye, and even to life. But I could not move him from his conviction that there was nothing in it, and the sight could be restored. Of course I refused to prescribe or to take any responsibility, and he left me. Two weeks afterwards he returned, with fearful swelling of the eye and face, excruciating pain, and commencing rigidity of the muscles of the jaw. In this extreme condition, hopeless as it was, he begged for enucleation. The operation was very difficult, and when at last the optic nerve was embraced by the scissors, they would not close. After much trouble, however, I succeeded in removing the eye. The large scale which I here show you, was found embraced by the wounded sclerotic, one end projecting backwards by the side of the optic nerve. The tetanus went on, as I expected, and after the most fearful sufferings I ever witnessed, the poor victim died, two weeks after the operation.

Another somewhat similar case was operated by my associate, Dr. S. C. Ayres, on the 10th of last April. Immediately after enucleation the ball was opened and examined. To our surprise no foreign body was found. A cicatrix, three lines in length, was detected in the sclerotic just below the optic nerve, through which it had passed out of the eye into the orbit. His socket was at once examined by the operator's finger, and the end of the foreign body distinctly felt wedged back into the apex. By a good deal of trouble it was seized and removed by the forceps, and you will see for yourselves its character. It is ⅝ of an inch in length and ⅜ in breadth, and somewhat like a piece of knife-blade.

I have, several times, enucleated eyes where the sight had been destroyed by bird shot, and where none were found in the globe, but distinct cicatrices of entrance and of exit. Such shot, or bullets, may sojourn in the socket perfectly harmless. In one instance, however, I saw an aneurism of the ophthalmic artery develop some months after such an injury. Occasionally a penetrating body or a shot spares the eye-ball but plunges behind it and wounds the optic nerve, causing instant loss of sight.

The sudden loss of sight from a penetrating wound of the orbit—the eye-ball itself having escaped injury—would thus admit of explanation. I once saw a young man who had fallen from a load of hay on the sharp, slender tine of a steel fork. He jerked it out, with some difficulty, but never saw light afterwards. When I examined him many years afterwards, I found the cicatrix in the upper lid, but no trace of injury to the globe. On ophthalmoscopic examination, I found nothing but extreme white atrophy of the optic nerve. It is almost certain that the nerve had been wounded, perhaps severed, by the fork.

A still more interesting case occurred in my practice, a few months ago. An old gentleman received an accidental discharge of bird shot in his face, with immediate total extinction of sight in both eyes. Two days after the accident I saw him and found, briefly, as follows: Right eye collapsed and riddled by shot, and numerous marks of others that had entered the face and lids of same side. The left side of the face showed only one mark of a shot in the lower lid, opposite the edge of the bony orbit. The pupil was largely dilated and fixed, with bare perception of light. Otherwise the eye was intact and the ophthalmoscope revealed absolutely nothing wrong. The disc appeared natural in all respects, and moderate pressure with the finger on the globe produced the usual visible pulsations of the arteries on its surface, showing that the main retinal artery, as it enters the trunk of the nerve a little back of the globe and follows in its axis to the interior of the eye, had not been injured. I diagnosed injury of the optic nerve some distance behind the globe, back of the point where it receives the artery. He suffered great pain in the right eye, for which I was induced at last to enucleate it. One shot was found in the bottom of the vitreous, but the others had passed entirely through into the orbit. He has been altogether free from pain since. The vision of the left eye gradually returned so that he can now see to walk about, recognize people, and read large print. The optic nerve shows moderate white atrophy.

An enumeration of all the *kinds* of foreign bodies that have been known to penetrate the eye, would be an impossible task. The most common are pieces of metal, percussion caps, stone, wood and shot. Sometimes we are surprised to find the foreign body very different from what we had expected from the history of the accident and the nature of the wound, or cicatrix. For instance, a little boy, five years old, was amusing himself by exploding caps, laying them on the pavement and striking them with a stone. A fragment struck the inner segment of the cornea and made a wound about one line in length. For some days he did not suffer much pain, and his physician thought the injury was not serious. At length, the inflammation and pain increasing, he was brought to me. The iris was discolored and pressed forward almost in contact with the cornea. The lens was opaque. The foreign body had evidently passed through the cornea, the iris, and into or through the lens. It was not possible to detect it. I enucleated the eye expecting, of course, to find a piece of a cap in it. After severing the recti muscles I passed my finger behind the globe, to luxate it. The pressure caused the corneal wound to open and the soft opaque lens escaped from the eye. I caught it, fortunately, and dropped it into the basin. On finishing the operation and opening the eye very carefully, I found no piece of cap. The lens in the basin was then examined and a small piece, not of the cap, but of *stone*, was found in it.

Another time, an eye had been extinguished by the sudden discharge of a gun-cartridge. The evidences of penetration and the presence of a foreign body deep in the eye, were clear. I discovered in the enucleated eye a piece of *pearl!* On careful inquiry, the patient stated that he was foolish enough to strike the cartridge with his pearl-handle knife. It exploded, and all he ever saw of the knife was the piece of pearl found in the vitreous.

Another man, while handling some pieces of wood, felt something, he does not know what, strike his left eye. It produced a triangular incised wound of the cornea, injured the lens, and caused cataract. Sight was lost at once, and for seven weeks he suffered constant pain. At that time the cornea was flattened, opaque in the centre, and apparently drawn down by the cicatrization; ball tender to the touch over the ciliary region; sclerotic and ciliary zone intensely injected. On removal, the vitreous was found liquid; retina in position, but in thickened, opaque folds. Corresponding to the corneal wound, a cicatricial tense ridge, or band, running across the ciliary processes, and having a firm, fibrous feeling and resistance. Within this citatrix was included an *eye-lash*, lying in the direction of the citatrix, with the bulbous end farthest from the cornea. Nothing else foreign was found. The wounding body had carried the cilia in and left it, after rebounding.

The presence of a foreign substance remaining in the ball, after penetration, increases the gravity of the case more or less, according to its nature, size, greater· or less roughness and especially its position. A small, smooth body in the vitreous may become encysted and remain harmless. Indeed this may, but rarely, occur, when it is in the iris, retina or choroid. In such instances it is nearly always resented, and keeps up endless trouble and never ceasing danger to the fellow eye. When fixed in or near the ciliary region, as they most frequently are, there is certainty of trouble sooner or later, and great danger of sympathetic ophthalmia in the other eye. It is in the lens perhaps, where extraneous bodies are longest tolerated after producing cataract. But eventually it may escape from the lens and produce violent and destructive reaction. A man while opening a keg of paint in April, 1875, with a hammer and chisel, felt something strike his brow, bringing a drop of blood. At the same moment a stinging sensation was noticed in the eye. There was no pain following the accident, and he insists that the sight remained perfectly good up to three weeks before I saw him, which was over a year. At that time, May 22, 1876, he could only count fingers at 3½ feet. There was cataract but without complete saturation. Deep in the lens was seen a shiny small piece of metal. In the anterior capsule was a visible wound with a tuft of lens substance protruding through it into the aqueous, and undergoing absorption. In the cornea a small scar was found where the metal had entered. He called to consult us about the failing sight. I advised him to wait a few weeks, as he was suffering no pain. There were no urgent symptoms. I believed that the absorption, through the rent in the capsule, would go on, and eventually the piece would come forward and be more easily and certainly removed with the lens. On Monday morning last he returned, having suffered intense pain for the previous ten days. As I feared, the foreign body had come forward, out of the lens and fallen into the anterior chamber. It was very small, but distinctly visible, lying in the lower rim of the anterior chamber. Under ether, I made a careful incision at the sclero-corneal junction close in front of it. The corresponding part of the iris was then drawn out and snipped off, the piece of metal coming out with it. It was not larger than half a pins head. I have another case under observation where a piece of metal of much larger size and of crescentic shape, penetrated the lens some years ago and still remains there,—the whole opaque lens substance now being liquid. The foreign body moves freely around in the closed capsule, according to the position of the head, always gravitating to the most dependent part. Little by little the fluid lens substance will be absorbed and the capsule will close in more and more on the foreign body, limiting its excursions. What will become of it, I hope to live long enough to see. It will probably cut through the capsule and fall into the chamber, some fine day. He suffers no inconvenience from it, except the blindness.

On Monday last a young man was brought to me suffering severely from an eye that had been injured, ten days previously, by the explosion of a mineral-water bottle, which he held in his hand. He felt a sharp sting in the eye, followed by bleeding. For the next twenty-four hours he did not suffer much, and could see large objects. Severe pain then set in; sight was extinguished, and he came to me in that condition. There was a cicatrix in the lower lid about a quarter of an inch long, just below the margin, and occupying its entire thickness. In the lower part of the sclerotic, through the ciliary region, exactly corresponding to the scar in the lid, was a penetrating wound a quarter of an inch long with two little radiating branches. The pupil was largely dilated, and the fundus of the eye showing a marked yellowish reflex, indicating extensive suppurative cheroiditis. I felt very confident that a large piece of glass was in the eye, but the turbidness of the vitreous prevented our seeing it. Enucleation was performed. There was extensive suppuration in the vitrous extending from the sclerotic wound across the ciliary body, with neuro-retinitis in a most intense form. The optic disc was greatly swollen, completely obscuring the vessels, and presenting the characteristic appearances so well known to ophthalmoscopists, of neuritis; but no foreign body was found in the eye. A long, slender, wedge-shaped piece of the bottle had passed through the lid, deep into the eye-ball, and then rebounded.

REPORT ON

Human Vaccine, Vaccino-Syphilis and Animal Vaccine,

WITH LETTERS FROM

Hebra, Sigmund, Seaton, M. Guerin, Zeissl, Neu-

mann and Widerhofer,

BY

WILLIAM B. DAVIS, A. M., M. D.,

Professor Materia Medica, Miami Medical College, Cincinnati, O.

REPORT ON

HUMAN VACCINE, VACCINO-SYPHILIS AND ANIMAL VACCINE,

WITH LETTERS FROM

Hebra. Sigmumd, Seaton, M. Guerin, Zeisal, Neumann and Widerhofer,

BY

WILLIAM B. DAVIS, A. M., M. D.,

Professor Materia Medica, Miami Medical College, Cincinnati.

In the year 1870, I had the honor of presenting a report on Vaccination to the Ohio State Medical Society, which considered in extenso the following questions:

1. *The Alleged Degeneration of the Humanized Vaccine Lymph.*

2. *Vaccinal Syphilis.*

3. *Animal Vaccine.*

Six years have elapsed since then, during which time Animal Vaccine has been very extensively used in Europe, and, if we can judge from the advertisements in our medical and lay journals, and the circulars forwarded to the members of our profession, it has also been used to some extent in our country. This being the case, a large amount of important evidence has accumulated on this subject, which will be of interest to the whole profession.

The use of Animal Vaccine is predicated upon the theory that Human Vaccine has degenerated, or that it is capable of transmitting syphilis, or upon both of these causes.   These are grave and weighty allegations, which have had more or less currency since vaccination has come into general use, and make it necessary, every few years, for the profession to carefully review the grounds for its faith in Jennerian vaccine.

Interested parties, having Animal Vaccine for sale, and the legitimate discussion of the subject in our journals, have sufficiently unsettled our profession to make a general review of the subject at this time a matter of interest. In view of this, last March I wrote letters to a number of the leading physicians of Europe, soliciting their opinions on the subject and the several questions involved in it. Their replies, however, were so slow in coming—and some are not yet received—that I find myself on the eve of the session of the State Society without time to prepare such a report as I had contemplated.   Nevertheless, the eminent gentlemen who have kindly responded to my inquiries, are so well known and highly honored, that their opinions on these important questions will be highly valued: therefore, I submit them with but few comments, further, than to group their opinions on each of the three questions.

The letters received are from Hebra, Seaton, Sigmund, M. Guerin, Neumann, Zeissl and Widerhofer.

I. *The Alleged Degeneration of Humanized Vaccine Lymph.*

All of the above mentioned authorities agree that the Humanized Vaccine Lymph has not degenerated; that when properly used it is as perfect in all of its manifestations and protective power as at the time of its origin.   Hebra, Neumann and Sigmund refer to " *The Foundling Hospital*" and the principal *Vaccine Institute of Vienna*, where the lymph used "has been carried down without interruption from the first vaccinations at the beginning of the present century; and now, after seventy years, this matter still 'takes' just as well as before, and its protective action against variola is as complete as that of lymph, which has, in the meantime, been derived from fresh inoculations with matter taken from the udder of the cow." Mr. Seaton makes refer- ence to the "National Vaccine Establishment" of Eng- land, where Jennerian lymph has been successively used by arm to arm vaccination for over seventy years, and the results are as perfect now as in the days of Jenner. All of them, directly or indirectly, insist that knowledge, skill and carefulness are necessary for the proper perform- ance of vaccination. A number of them speak of what they term the "culture" of the vaccine. Probably Mr. Dar- win would call it the survival of the fittest. M. Guerin says, "the culture of vaccine must not be confounded with the choice of vaccine; it is something more than that." I presume it means lymph from the most perfectly developed vesicle—before the stage of areola—from the arm of a child in perfect health and known to be free from all constitutional taint, transplanted to one equally sound and healthy.

The Imperial Academy of Medicine (Paris), after a thorough investigation of the two vaccines (human and animal), adopted the following resolution: •

"That human, or Jennerian vaccine, whose efficacy and benefit a long and vast experience has established, does not appear susceptible of losing its virtues, but transiently, and in consequence of a want of care in the choice of the vaccinifer, or of the neglect of the rules for a good vaccination. * * * The Jennerian vaccine is entitled to the continued confidence of science and of the public." [See "M," page 84.]

Sigmund says cultivation alone is not sufficient for a good vaccination. The operation demands knowledge, experience and skill; hence it should never be performed by inexperienced or ignorant persons, but be carefully done by the most competent and conscientious physicians.

Mr. Seaton says, "there should be an increase of care both in choice of vaccinifers and in performing the operation, especially in avoiding any blood in the lymph used, and in scrupulous observance of Jenner's 'Golden Rule': to take lymph always before the vesicle has reached the stage of areola." In England there are Educational Vaccine Stations, established by the Government, where physicians are instructed in the art of vaccinating, and a Certificate of Proficiency is given to those who attend and prove themselves worthy. All public vaccinators must have them. [See Educational Vaccine Stations, "K," page 81.]

2. *Vaccinal Syphilis. Will Lymph from a True Jennerian Vesicle Transmit Syphilis?*

Neumann says: "I know of vaccinal syphilis only from the literature on the subject. In my experience as a practitioner of medicine, I have never met with a case." [See "A.," page 66.]

Hebra says: "No other morbid conditions or dyscrasia can be introduced by vaccination. No one, when he has been inoculated with syphilitic poison, fancies that he may, at the same time, have acquired scrofula or gout, and yet it is just as probable that this should occur, as that any other disease should be conveyed by vaccination." [See papers "B" and "C," pages 66-67.]

Zeissl says: "Syphilitic infection, by means of vaccination, can only take place when the material used does not consist of pure vaccine lymph, but is mixed with syphilitic tissues or blood." He also states that "he has observed that *vaccine lymph taken from syphilitic children did not produce syphilis in those vaccinated with it when only pure lymph, entirely free from blood or other tissue elements, was used.*" [See letter "D," page 68.]

For Instructions of Privy Council, concerning Properly Performed Vaccinations, see "L," page 82.

M. Guerin says: "It is not demonstrated that human vaccination produces syphilis; on the contrary, it is demonstrated that it is always possible to prevent this dreadful adulteration." He states "that it is possible for certain eruptions and ulcerations to follow the most innocent vaccine, and the cases presented by the Commissioners of the French Academy of Medicine as examples of vaccinal syphilis were not syphilis, but resulted from simple complications and alterations of the vaccine, all of which could be avoided by proper care." [See paper "E," page 69.]

Widerhofer says: "The transmission of syphilis by means of vaccination can be avoided if all precautionary measures are strictly observed." In all cases of vaccinal syphilis which he has known of, one or more of the necessary precautions have been neglected. [See letter "F," page 72.]

Sigmund states: "That in his whole professional career, extending as far back as the year 1837, he has seen but three cases of undoubted syphilis which were claimed to have been transmitted by vaccination. No reliable history or data, however, could be obtained in these cases." According to his own experience, "syphilis never occurred when pure vaccine lymph was used and the operation was performed by an expert physician." He states that "*no case of syphilis has ever been transmitted by lymph obtained from the Vaccine Institute of Vienna, which has been in operation since the discovery of vaccination.*" "Instead of distrusting vaccination," he adds: "it is best to avoid all possible sources of error and danger, and have the operation performed by the most competent and conscientious physicians." [See letter "G," page 74.]

Mr. Seaton refers to some cases reported by Mr. Hutchinson, and says they "seem to me to have been undoubtedly cases of what is termed vaccino-syphilis; i. e., of the introduction of the syphilitic poison in the act of vaccination. Facts left no doubt on my mind that the lymph employed in these vaccinations was contaminated with blood, and that the infection was conveyed by the blood." About the same time, he saw another case, in which there was a strong presumption that syphilis had been introduced in the same way. He adds: "I know of no other cases, and the interest that the above cases excited, and the lookout that has been kept on all sides for similar cases since (1871), render it most probable that had any occurred, I should not have remained ignorant of them." He says the few cases on record "are accidental cases—not only of extreme rarity, but in my opinion avoidable. The true lesson of those cases is, an increase of care, both in choice of vaccinifers and in performance of the operation, especially as regards the latter, in avoiding any blood contamination (however slight) of the lymph employed." [See letter "H," page 76.]

The two series of cases of vaccinal syphilis of Mr. Hutchinson, referred to by Mr. Seaton, and published in "The Medico-Chirurgical Transactions" for 1871; vol. LIV., page 317. [See extracts from said Report "I." on page 78.] This report was read before the Royal Medical and Chirurgical Society of London, and referred to a special committee of four for examination and report. On May 16th, 1871, they made a detailed report, in the course of which they state that they had seen, in company of Mr. Hutchinson, the following cases: "The vaccinifer of the first series of cases reported on April 25th, and three persons (cases 1, 2, 3) who were vaccinated from this child." After a description of each case, they say: "From the foregoing account, it will be seen that neither the vaccinifer, nor any one of the three cases vaccinated from it, presented any symptoms of constitutional syphilis at the time of our examination."

Concerning the second series of cases, they say there was evidence of constitutional syphilis in three cases. "As to the method in which vaccination was performed in these cases and the character of the fluid inoculated—whether lymph, blood, or both—we could obtain no satisfactory evidence."

It will be interesting in this connection to refer to Mr. Simon's views on vaccinal syphilis. On everything which pertains to vaccination there is no greater authority. They will be found in his Twelfth Report as Medical Officer of the Privy Council [extracts from which are published on page 80 of this report, "J"]. He says: "If ordinary current vaccination propagates syphilis, where is the syphilis that it propagates? Who sees it? The experience of this department is an entire blank on the subject. * * * Our national vaccine establishment has been in existence for more than sixty years, vaccinating at its own stations every year several thousands of applicants, and transmitting to other stations supplies of lymph, with which every year very many other thousands are vaccinated, who, in their turn, become sources of vaccination to others; but this vast experience does not, so far as I can ascertain, include knowledge of even one solitary case in which it has been alleged that the lymph has communicated syphilis." Sigmund, it will be remembered, states in his letter that "syphilis has never been transmitted by the humanized lymph obtained from the *principal vaccine institute of Vienna*, which has been in operation since the discovery of vaccination.

III.—ANIMAL VACCINE—COW POX LYMPH.

PROF. WIDERHOFER, in his letter, defines the different kinds of Vaccine Lymph as follows:

1. *Original Cow Pox Lymph*, is lymph taken from a pustule, *spontaneously* developed in a cow.
2. *Regenerated Cow Pox Lymph*, is lymph taken from a pustule artificially produced in a cow; (*a*) by inoculation with original cow pox lymph, or as is usually done, (*b*) by inoculation with humanized vaccine lymph.

3. Regenerated Cow Pox Lymph, after having passed through the human system *once* becomes *Humanized Cow Pox Lymph*.

4. In its further passage through the human organism, it becomes the usual *Humanized Vaccine Lymph*.

1. With original Cow Pox Lymph he has seen numerous vaccinations made in children, but in only one case with perfect success. In this case the inflammatory action was very severe, but otherwise its course was normal. With every successive transmission through the human system it becomes more certain in its effects and milder in its action.

2. Regenerated Cow Pox Lymph, he says, is very uncertain in its action, and is not apt to take at all unless it is directly; and without delay, transplanted from the animal to the human, and even then it is not so certain as the Humanized Lymph. Transporting, or keeping even for a few hours, not only weakens its effectiveness, but in most cases renders it inert.

3. Humanized Cow Pox Lymph has much greater protective power, when it has once become effective in the human economy. If any one has scruples about vaccinating with human lymph, he says they will apply with equal force against the Humanized Cow Pox Lymph. [Letter " F "]

NEUMAN says he prefers humanized to Cow Pox Lymph, when proper precautions are used. He says the Vaccine Institute, of Vienna, furnishes the strongest testimony in its favor.

HEBRA says Humanized Lymph should be used for vaccination in preference to that derived directly from the cow. For the former takes easily, is followed by a comparatively slight reaction, gives as complete protection against variola, and is easily obtained ; while the latter is uncertain in its effects and gives rise to much more intense inflammatory action.

M. GUERIN says that animal vaccine has not the same elements of action and does not produce the same physiological results as the human vaccine. It does not give the same protection against variola. Vaccination direct from the heifer was almost universally adopted in Paris in 1864. In 1869-70 a fearful epidemic of small-pox raged in that city. M. Guerin says that it is generally believed that the dreadful ravages of that epidemic of small-pox were due to the substitution of animal vaccine for the Jennerian.

Concerning the *inocuous* character of animal vaccine he says : "If it does not transmit Syphilis, facts well authenticated have sadly demonstrated that it does produce *Charbon* and *Typhus*." Dr. Beaupoil, of Ingrande, in his report on practical vaccination, in 1871, cites a case of a Counselor of the Court of Paris, who died of *Charbon* resulting from an inoculation with vaccine direct from the heifer. Two other cases of the same disease following animal vaccination occurred in England. He says emphatically, "animal vaccine is dead."

The French Academy of Medicine has declared that the largest liberty shall be allowed for the demonstration of the value of animal vaccine, but this liberty must not be exercised at the expense of the human vaccine, for the latter is entitled to the continued confidence of science and the public. [See "M," page 84.]

SIGMUND makes no mention of animal vaccine, and ZEISSL says : "As to the merits of direct or indirect vaccination I am free to confess that I am not an authority and my experience will not warrant me in expressing an opinion." So far, however, as vaccinal syphilis is concerned, he says it can be prevented by using lymph direct from the cow, as Syphilis is a disease peculiar to the human family.

MR. SEATON, Medical Inspector of the Privy Council, England, in the autumn of 1869 visited Paris, Brussels, Rotterdam and Amsterdam, where animal vaccine was extensively used, for the purpose of investigating the following points : (1) "The transmissibility of cow pox, unimpaired, from animal to animal ; (2) the character and course of the affection produced on the human subject by this animal lymph ; (3) the success attending the employment of this lymph on the human subject ; and (4) the preservability of the lymph."

His report shows (1) "That apparently even able and painstaking operators may find it impossible to transmit successive vaccinations from calf to calf without very frequent recurrence of failures and interruptions ; (2) that the transference of the infection from the calf to the human subject, even under the most favorable circumstances, (i. e. by experienced operators and with lancet direct from calf to arm) has in it such risks for failure, that the proportion of unsuccess was nearly twenty times as great as the ordinary arm-to-arm vaccination ; and (3) that the calf lymph, as compared with ordinary lymph, is peculiarly apt to spoil with keeping, and in the form of tube-preserved lymph can so little be relied on, that the Rotterdam establishment, in distributing supplies of lymph, now uses only lymph from the human subject." His report can be found in the 12th Report of the Privy Council, (1870). In reply to my inquiry whether he had any information which would incline him to modify or change the opinions expressed in his Report, he says: "nothing has altered my opinion expressed in the Report to which you refer, of what it (animal vaccination) really is, and of the inadvisibility of the practice. On the contrary, there has been, since I wrote, an accumulation of independent testimony, showing the large relative amount of failure which attend it, which strengthens my views that its general adoption (if indeed it were practicable) would greatly weaken our defenses against small-pox. I think it would be a very serious thing if we were frightened into such a measure by the occurrence of a few accidental cases (of vaccino syphilis), not only of extreme rarity, but in my opinion, avoidable."

I think the above statements will justify the following

CONCLUSIONS.

1. *Humanized vaccine lymph has not degenerated;* on the contrary, it is conclusively proven that when proper care is exercised it is as perfect to-day, in all its manifestations, and as complete a protection against small-pox, as in the days of Jenner.

2. *Syphilis cannot be transmitted by humanized vaccine lymph* unless syphilitic pus, tissues, or blood be mixed with the vaccine lymph. When proper precautions are used, such contaminations can be avoided.

3. *Animal vaccine—particularly cow-pow lymph and re-generated cow-pox lymph—*is very difficult to take, unduly severe in its action when it does take, will not bear transportation or preservation with any degree of certainty, and does not afford the same degree of protection against small pox as humanized vaccine lymph.

Whilst it may not transmit syphilis, *it has transmitted charbon and typhus,* which are more dangerous to life than syphilis.

APPENDIX.

A.

LETTER FROM ISIDOR NEUMAN, M. D.

K. K. Prof. an der Wiener Universitat, Primararzt der K. K. Allg.
Krankenhaus in Wein, etc., etc.

VIENNA, 1, Rothenthurm strasse, 29, May 9, 1876.

Honored Colleague:

I hope that I shall not be too late with my reply to the questions addressed me by yourself, regarding the transmission of syphilis through vaccination.

I only know of vaccinal syphilis from the literature on the subject. In my experience as a practitioner of medicine, I have never met with a case.

When all proper precautions are used, such as are required by our laws, I prefer humanized lymph to cow-pox lymph. Our foundling house, which is connected with the principal vaccine institute, furnishes the strongest testimony in favor of it.

The children used for propagating the lymph should be over three months old.

I remain with the highest regard,
Your colleague,
ISADOR NEUMAN.

Prof. Wm. B. Davis.

———— o ————

B.

LETTER FROM FERDINAND HEBRA, M. D.

Prof. fur Dermatologie an der Universatat, Primararzt der Abstheilung
fur Hautkrankheiten in K. K. Allg. Kranken-
haus in Wein, etc., etc.

VIENNA, ix., Marianneng, 10, May 7th, 1876.

Honored Sir:

On page 240 of the second edition of my "Manual of Skin Diseases," you will find my views concerning your questions, expressed in extenso. There I set forth more fully than I can in this brief note, that I regard humanized vaccine lymph preferable to lymph taken directly from the cow. As regards vaccino-syphilis, a knowledge of the character of both efflorescences will prevent the physician from confounding a vaccine pustule with a syphilitic one.

Again referring you to my " Manual,"

I am with distinguished esteem,

Yours respectfully,

HEBRA.

Prof. Wm. B. Davis, M. D., Miami Medical College, Cincinnati, U. S. A.

————o————

C.

Professor Hebra's views, to which reference is made in his letter: [" Manual of Skin Diseases," 2d. ed., page 240. Publication of the Sydenhaus Society, vol. 1, page 274.]

When a human being is inoculated with lymph taken immediately from one of the lower animals, the operation is less certain to succeed than when the lymph is merely transferred from one to another. Moreover, in the former case, the pustules which are produced are attended by far more severe symptoms of reaction than when lymph has been previously *humanized.*

These observations suggested the further inquiry whether more perfect security from small pox is offered by vaccinating with lymph taken directly from the cow, or by employing vaccine matter which has already been transmitted in succession through several human beings. We are enabled to answer this question with the utmost certainty, by the results obtained at the principal vaccine institution at Vienna. Some of the lymph used in this establishment has been carried down without interruption from the first vaccinations practiced by De Carro at the beginning of the present century ; and now, at the end of seventy years, this matter still " takes " just as well as before, and its protective action against variola is as complete as that of lymph, which has in the meantime been derived from fresh inoculations with matter taken from the udder of the cow. It appears to me, therefore, that lymph which has already been humanized, should at the present day be used for vaccination rather than that derived directly from the cow. For the former takes easily, is followed by a comparatively slight reaction, and is readily obtained ; while the latter is uncertain in its effects and gives rise to much more intense inflammatory action. The principal reason which has induced people to prefer original cow-pox lymph to that which has passed through the human system, has been the fear that other diseases besides vaccinia might possibly be transferred to the patient by vaccination. But experience has now shown that no other morbid conditions or dyscrasiae can be thus introduced. Indeed, no one, when he ·has unintentionally become inoculated with the syphilitic poison, fancies that he may at the same time have acquired scrofula or gout ; but it is just as probable that this should occur, as that any other disease should be conveyed by vaccination besides the mild form of small pox, which it is the object of the operation to transmit. This question has in fact been submitted to direct experiment by using for inoculation a mixture of chancrous pus and vaccine virus ; the result of employing this combination being that sometimes a chancre was produced, sometimes a vaccine vesicle, but never any modification of them or any third affection."

———— o ————

D.

LETTER FROM HERMAN ZEISSL, M. D.,

K K , Professor an der Wiener Universitat, Primararzt der K. K. Allg. Krankenhauses in Wein, etc., etc.

Vienna, Tiefen-Graben, 10, May 14, 1876.

Esteemed Professor :

With great pleasure I undertake to answer the questions addressed me in your honored letter. Permit me to say—

1. Several years since I stated in my *Manuel* that "Lues" cannot be transmitted by vaccination, unless syphilitic tissue elements have been mixed with the vaccine lymph. A syphilitic infection, by means of vaccination, can only take when the vaccine material used does not consist of *pure vaccine lymph*, but is mixed with broken down tissues of

syphilitic efflorescences, or with particles of blood of syphilitic patients, or when the instrument used for vaccinating is contaminated with syphilitic virus.

2. Just as little as any toxic material transforms itself into another virus, just so little does the vaccine lymph transform itself into syphilitic virus by its passage through a syphilitic organism.

3. I have seen many children affected with latent syphilis, in whom vaccination ran its course as perfectly as though they were entirely free from syphilitic taint.

4. I have also noticed, that vaccinations made with vaccine virus taken from syphilitic children, did not produce syphilis in the vaccinated *when only the clear vaccine lymyh, entirely free of blood and other tissue elements, was transplanted.*

5. As to the question of the comparative merits of direct or indirect vaccination, I am free to confess that I am not an authority, and my experience would not warrant me in expressing an opinion. So far as vaccinal syphilis is concerned, I can say, with great positiveness, that it most certainly can be prevented by using lymph direct from the cow, and not the arm to arm vaccination ; because my experience leads me to believe that " Lues" is a disease peculiar to the human organism, and does not show itself in warm-blooded animals in the same manner as in human beings. Very Respectfully,

ZEISSL.

Wm. B. Davis, M. D., Prof. Materia Medica, Miami Medical College, Cincinnati, U. S. A.

———o———

E.

LETTER FROM M. JULES GUERIN, M. D.,

A Distinguished Member of the Imperial Academy of Medicine.

PARIS, April 20, 1876.

My Dear Colleague :

At the very moment your kind letter arrived, I was busy superintending the publication of my discourses in the Academy of Medicine, during the discussion on *Animal Vaccination* and *Vaccinal Syphilis.* I can not reply better to

6

your inquiries.than by sending you the proofs of my five discourses, together with the preface. Please accept them,
with my compliments, for your learned Society.   As
you will see in my preface, the work will embrace a historical
sketch of vaccination ; but as it will be one or two months
before this part is completed, I shall forward you what I
have, in order that you may not be retarded with your work.

Allow me to assure you, my learned colleague, of my most
distinguished considerations.

JULES GUERIN.

Prof. Wm. B. Davis.

————o————

EXTRACTS FROM M. GUERIN'S DISCOURSES.

Below will be found extracts from M. Guerin's discourses, bearing on the questions under discussion.   His
work is probably the latest one published on the subject,
and as Animal Vaccination has been used almost to the
exclusion of Human Vaccine, in Paris, since 1864, and
M. Guerin has been an interested and an intelligent
observer during all this period, his observations will be of
great interest.

On page 7 he says:

My thesis comprehends the four propositions which follow :
1.   It is not demonstrated that Human Vaccine has degenerated, at least in a general or absolute manner. On the contrary, it is demonstrated that it is possible to assure the
preservation of the properties which it had at its origin.
2.   It is not demonstrated that Human Vaccination produces vaccinal syphilis.   On the contrary, it is demonstrated
that it is always possible to prevent this dreadful adulteration.
3.   It is not demonstrated that Animal Vaccine possesses
the elements of action, and produces physiological effects
identical with those of Human Vaccine.   On the contrary,
it is demonstrated that the two vaccines possess elements of
action, and produce physiological results, entirely different.
4.   Lastly : There is only presumptive evidence in favor
of the protecting virtues of Animal Vaccine. On the contrary, it is proven most conclusively that the Human Vaccine
remains always almost an absolute protection against variola.

1. *The Alleged Degeneration of Human Vaccine.* Under this head he says the genuine lymph has not ceased to be what it was originally; it has remained identically the same. The properties and results have never been modified but temporarily and exceptionally, and then only because of a modification of the conditions and circumstances which surround it. These modifications and variations are attributable as much to the condition of the person vaccinated as to the state of the vaccine. Under these conditions it may appear temporarily modified and weakened; but as soon as the conditions are more favorable and the subject better, it manifests all of its original qualities. The Jennerian vaccine will never degenerate if we make what we have called the culture of vaccine; this must not be confounded with choice of vaccine; it is something more than that.

2. *Vaccinal Syphilis.* This question has received a solution as decisive as the first one. It is well known that the most innocent vaccine may be followed by ulcerations which resemble syphilitic and other eruptions, and it is well established that the abnormal eruptions—the so-called secondary or tertiary symptoms of Syphilis were but accidents of ordinary vaccine. The cases which were produced during the discussion in the Academy, as well as others which have occurred since, were mistakes. The symptoms which were taken to be secondary or tertiary Syphilis, were found afterwards to be alterations of the pustule or insignificant eruptions of pemphigus or some other eruption. The cases of *Morbihan*, presented by the Commissioners of the Academy as examples of vaccinal Syphilis, interpreted as they should be, and connected with other analagous cases—those of Albi, for example—have come from simple complications and alterations of the vaccine.

3. *Animal Vaccine.* Having shown that the Jennerian vaccine does not degenerate, and that it does not form impure alliances, it remains for us to consider the graver question, viz: the prophylactic virtue of the two vaccines. The Jennerian vaccine is fortified by a vast experience which becomes stronger every day, but experience is never complete, hence I proposed that we should make comparative experiments, by re-vaccinating, at different periods, children who had been vaccinated with two viruses. The experiments sufficed up to a certain point. A number of those recently vaccinated with animal vaccine took variola a little while after their vaccination. But these

scattered cases do not have the demonstrative value of an experiment instituted *ad hoc*. There is a test so grave that one scarcely dares mention it, which establishes beyond a doubt the inferiority of animal vaccine, viz : the dreadful ravages produced by the recent epidemic of small-pox in Paris are generally believed to be due to the substitution of animal vaccine for the Jennerian.   *   *   *   The humanized cow pox is open to the same objection, for the mixture of the two vaccines is an adulteration which annihilates the true virus.   *   *   *   But it is claimed for animal vaccine that it is inocuous—that it cannot convey any other disease but vaccinia. If it does not transmit Syphilis, facts perfectly authenticated, have sadly demonstrated that it does produce Charbon and Typhus. Dr. Beaupoil, of Ingrande, in his report on practical vaccination, in 1871, cites a case of a Counselor of the Court of Paris, who died of Charbon, resulting from an inoculation with vaccine direct from the heifer. Two other cases of the same disease have occured in England. They were reported in the " Union Medicale," April, 1873.

———o———

[F.]

LETTER FROM H. WIDERHOFER, M. D.

Prof. an der Wiener Universität ; Director des St. Annen Kinder Spitals, etc., etc.

VIENNA, I Habsburger, Gasse 9, May 8th, 1876.

Respected Colleague :

I should sincerely regret if my answer to your kind letter would reach you too late for your purposes.

Before replying to your questions, I will define what I understand as to the different kinds of vaccine lymph.

1.   *Original Cow Pox Lymph,* is lymph taken from a pustule *spontaneously* developed in a cow.

2.   *Regenerated Cow Pox Lymph,* is lymph taken from a pustule artificially produced in a cow ; (*a*) by inoculation with original cow pox lymph (this would be the purest), or, as is usually done, (*b*) by inoculation with humanized vaccine lymph.

3. Regenerated Cow Pox Lymph, after having passed through the human system *once* becomes *Humanized Cow Pox Lymph*.

4. In its further passage through the human organism it becomes the usual *Humanized Lymph*.

With No. 1 original cow pox lymph I have seen numerous vaccinations made in children, but only in one case with perfect success. In this case the local reaction was very severe but otherwise its course was normal. With each successive transmission through the human system it becomes more certain in its effects and milder in its action.

With No. 2 *Regenerated Cow Pox Lymph* I have made very many vaccinations, and have not observed any material difference in its development and course from that of human vaccine lymph. I must add, however, that it is very uncertain in its action, and indeed it is not apt to take at all, unless it is directly, and without delay, transplanted from the animal to the human being, and even then it is not so certain as the human vaccine lymph. Transportation or preservation, even for a few hours, not only weakens its effectiveness, but, in most cases, renders it inert. With us the No. 3 humanized cow pox lymph is chiefly used for forwarding to points more or less remote.

Experience, which cannot be doubted, shows that this humanized lymph has much greater protective power, when it has once become effective in the human body, even though at first it may have been uncertain.

The unreliable results of No. 2, Regenerated lymph, makes its use a grave considertion in cases of re-vaccination, where successful results are always uncertain.

Now I come to your question, as to the possibility of conveying Syphilis by means of vaccination.

I fully coincide with the view that the transmission of Syphilis by means of vaccination with human lymph, and consequently with humanized cow pox, may, from all that is now known, be *avoided*, if all, yes *all* precautionary measures are strictly observed. In all cases of vaccino-syphilis which have become known to me up to this date, some one or more of the necessary precautions have been neglected. Very much to our regret, experience shows that such omissions are possible, and when they occur, syphilitic inoculation is apt to follow. In view of this, in my judgment, the preference must be given to the regenerated cow pox lymph.

No. 2 (*a*), although the result is less certain, I know of no advantage that the humanized cow pox lymph has, except that it is more certain in its results.   If any one has scruples about vaccinating with human lymph, they will apply with equal force against humanized cow pox lymph for it has also passed through the human system.

I shall be happy, honored colleague, if these lines will be of service to you.   Meanwhile,

I remain, with the highest esteem,

Your humble colleague,

PROF. DR. WIDERHOFER. ·

Prof. Wm. B. Davis, Miami Medical College, Cincinnati. U. S. A.

———o———

[G.] ·

LETTER FROM CARL LUDWIG SIGMUND, M. D.,

Ritter V. Ilanor, Professor an der Wiener Universitat, Primarzt der K.
K. Allg. Krankenhauses im Wien, etc., etc.

VIENNA, May 14th, 1876.

Dear Sir:

I received your letter of March 21st, on the 10th inst., and hasten to make the following reply :

1.   I have known of but three cases where syphilis was transmitted by vaccination, during my whole professional career, which extends back to the year 1837.   In each of these cases the lymph was taken from the arm of a child concerning whom no reliable data or history could be obtained.   Other children were vaccinated from them and they became sick, and a close inquiry left no doubt but that syphilis was transmitted to them.   No case of syphilis, however, has ever been produced by the lymph obtained from the *Vaccine Institute of Vienna.*   Here, it is well known, the Jennerian vaccine has been propagated by arm to arm vaccination, from the date of its discovery to the present day.

2.   As a set-off to the above cases, whose correctness I cannot doubt, I have seen very · many cases wherein it was charged that the vaccine lymph had transmitted syphilis.   A rigid examination, however, proved :   (1st) that in some of these cases there was no syphilis at all, nor any form of disease which could in any way warrant such a conclusion.

(2nd) In the majority there was syphilis, but the vaccine was not the cause of it. It was due to an hereditary taint and other sources quite independent of the vaccine lymph. I think a critical examination into all the factors and etiology will corroborate this statement everywhere.

3. In Italy, as well as this vicinity, I have seen many cases of vaccinations with regenerated cow pox lymph,—a process described more than two decades ago in St. Florian, near Gratz,—and have never seen syphilis transmitted by it, or heard of its occurrence elsewhere.

4. I have often vaccinated adults who had syphilis, with humanized lymph, and in every case the vaccine disease ran its course just the same as in those free from syphilis.

5. Mixtures of vaccine virus with the pus of venereal ulcers (contagious soft), produced pustules, which ran their course in one, two, three days, as simple pustulous dermatitis, followed by ulceration, from which fresh ulcers could be produced by inoculation. In 1859, for clinical and didactic purposes (in Gratiam Boeck), I had occasion to resort to syphilization, and the results often corroborated the above observations. It was interesting to observe that, when these same persons were vaccinated later, that is, re-vaccinated, some had finely developed vaccine pustules, while in others there was no result.

6. According to my observations, syphilis never occurred when pure vaccine lymph was used, and when the operation was performed by an expert physician.

It has been proposed in England, and suggested by myself (1864, Vienna Medical Wochenshrift, 53), that the vaccine lymph should be made the subject of the most careful cultivation, by taking it only from the healthiest children and transmitting it only to such children as have been known to be well for at least one year prior—" well," in the sense of being free from syphilitic taint. Some have thought that this lymph could be trusted in less experienced hands, but I assert the contrary ; for the operation requires skill, knowledge of the vaccinifer, and a judicious observation of the results. Great care must be taken when large numbers are vaccinated at the same time. Indeed, after every operation the instrument should be cleansed, as there is danger of vaccinating a syphilitic child and then a healthy child, and so on. Hence, the operation must be performed by skilled physicians in order to prevent such dangerous errors.

Vaccination, properly performed, is the surest safeguard against small-pox. In some European districts distrust has arisen, and, as a consequence, vaccination is less strenuously urged. In all such places small-pox is increasing rapidly, vide Vienna, etc., etc. Instead of distrusting vaccination, we had better avoid all possible sources of error and danger, and have the operation performed by the most competent and conscientious physicians.

I intentionally pass by hypothesis and theories; hence I have not touched upon the possibility of the vaccine lymph from a syphilitic patient, with or without blood, producing infection. And for the same reasons, have excluded other cachexia, or constitutional disorders.

I remain, with great esteem,
Your devoted colleague,
SIGMUND.

Prof. Wm. B. Davis.

————o————

. [H.]

LETTER FROM EDWARD C. SEATON, M. D.,

Medical Inspector of the Privy Council, England.

LOCAL GOVERNMENT BOARD,
WHITEHALL, LONDON, May 8, 1876. }

My Dear Sir:

I must express my great regret at having overlooked your letter of March 12th, which I had fully intended to have answered at the time. I hope that I am not now too late for your purpose.

You ask me two questions: (1) If I have any information which would incline me to modify, or change, the opinions which I expressed on animal vaccination in the report I made on the subject to the Privy Council, in 1869, and, (2) whether any well authenticated case of the in-vaccination of syphilis has come to my knowledge since the publication of Mr. Simons' 12th annual report to the Privy Council?

It will be most convenient to answer the latter question first:

In the transactions of the Royal Medical and Chirurgical Society, of London, for 1871, (which is doubtless accessible to you,) there is a report by Mr. Hutchinson, of two series of cases, of both of which I was cognizant, which seem to me to have been undoubtedly cases of what is termed vaccino-syphilis, viz : of the introduction of the syphilitic poison in the act of vaccination. Fact's left no doubt on my mind that the lymph employed in those vaccinations was contaminated with blood, and that the infection was conveyed by the blood. The cases occurred at the time of the small-pox panic, in 1871. About, but not exactly at the same time as above, I saw an isolated case in which there was strong presumption that the syphilis from which a young man was suffering, who had been re-vaccinated some weeks previous, had been introduced in the same way. I know of no other cases, and the interest that the above cases excited, and the look-out that has been kept on all sides for similar cases since, render it most probable that, had any occurred, I should not have remained ignorant of them. Several *alleged* cases since, have proved, on investigation, to be, every one of them, void of foundation.

With regard to the effect of these cases on my judgment as to animal vaccination, I am obliged to say that, while their occurrence made me wish that animal vaccination was other than it is, both as to facility of administration and as to effectiveness, it has not altered my opinion, expressed in the report to which you refer, of what it really is and of the inadvisibility of the practice. On the contrary, there has been, since I wrote, an accumulation of independent testimony showing the large relative amount of failure which attends it, which strengthens my views that its general adoption (if, indeed, it were practicable,) would greatly weaken our defenses against small-pox.

I think it would be a very serious thing if we were frightened into such a measure by the occurrence of a few accidental cases, not only of extreme rarity, but, in my opinion, avoidable. The true lesson of those cases is, an increase of care both in choice of vaccinifers and in performance of the operation, especially as regards the latter, in avoiding any blood contamination (however slight), of the lymph employed, and in scrupulous observance of Jenner's "Golden Rule," to take lymph always *before* the vesicle has reached the stage of areola.

Yours, very faithfully.
EDWARD C. SEATON.

Dr. Wm. B. Davis.

[I.]

CASES REFERRED TO IN MR. SEATON'S LETTER.

Extracts from a report entitled a " Report on Two Series of Cases, in which Syphilis was Communicated in the Practice of Vaccination," by Jonathan Hutchinson, F. R. C. S. (Medico-Chirurgical Transactions, 1871, *page* 317.)

FIRST SERIES OF CASES.

" *Synopsis :* Twelve persons, mostly young adults, vaccinated from a healthy-looking child. Satisfactory progress of the vaccination in all. Indurated chancres on the arms of ten of the vaccinated in the eighth week. Treatment by mercury in all. Rapid disappearance of the primary sores. Constitutional symptoms in four (4) of the patients in five (5) months after the vaccination. The vaccinifer showing condylomata at the age of six months."

SECOND SERIES OF CASES.

" *Synopsis:* Unquestionable symptoms of constitutional syphilis in nine children who had been vaccinated from the same patient. Suspicious symptoms in six others, and entire escape of a certain number. Vaccinifer a fine healthy-looking child, but with slight local symptoms indicative of inherited syphilis."

In the first series of cases, both the operator and the child's mother state that the vesicles from which the lymph was taken " bled somewhat." In the second series of cases, " no trustworthy evidence could be obtained as to whether blood was or was not transferred in the act of vaccination."

MR. HUTCHINSON'S CONCLUSIONS.

1. That the blood of a child suffering from inherited syphilis can, if inoculated, transmit the disease with great certainty.

2. That the result of such inoculation of blood will be an indurate chancre.

3. That if multiple inoculations be practiced, multiple chancres may be produced.

4. That a period of incubation between the inoculation and the first occurrence of induration about the prick will occur, during which the part may appear perfectly healthy.

5. That the period of incubation prior to the first specific induration will usually be about five weeks.

6. That it is quite possible for vaccine lymph and blood to be transferred at the same time, and for each to produce its specific results, the effects of the syphilitic inoculation occurring subsequently to those of vaccination.

7. That it is quite possible to vaccinate successfully from a syphilitic infant in the stage of utmost potency as regards its blood, without communicating syphilis.

The report of Mr. Hutchinson was read at the meeting of the Royal Medical and Chirurgical Society, and by it referred to a sub-committee. On May 16th, 1871, the committee reported that they had seen, in company with Mr. Hutchinson, the following cases :

"The vaccinifer of the first series of cases reported on April 25th, and three persons (cases 1, 2, 3) who were vaccinated from this child."

After a full description of each case, the report says :

"From the foregoing account, it will be seen that neither the vaccinifer, nor any one of the three cases vaccinated from it, presented any symptoms of constitutional syphilis at the time of our examination."

Concerning the second series of cases, the report says :

"In our opinion three cases present unequivocal evidence of constitutional syphilis, and we see no reason to doubt, from the appearances presented by the arms and from the history of the cases, that the disease had been conveyed by vaccination. As to the method in which vaccination was performed in these cases and the character of the fluid inoculated, whether lymph, blood, or both, we could obtain no satisfactory evidence." (Signed,)

SAMUEL WILKS,
WM. S. SAVORY,
GEO. G. GASCOYEN,
THOMAS SMITH.

[J.]

VACCINAL SYPHILIS—VIEWS OF JOHN SIMON,

Medical Officer of the Privy Council, England.

Mr. Simon, in his Twelfth Report to the Privy Council (1869, page 42), says:

"During the last sixty years the medical literature of Europe has gradually accumulated records of various occasions (I believe, in all, more than twenty), on which it has been definitely imputed to a vaccinator that he had made syphilitic inoculations." Ten of these cases were produced by one man, and " he thinks it certain that the so-called vaccinator really did, somehow or other, produce the result which was imputed to him." * * * " The vaccinator's declaration of blamelessness must, from the nature of the case, be almost valueless * * he unawares did some thoughtless or slovenly act which mixed syphilitic and vaccine contagia on his lancet, or substituted the former contagium for the latter." Of the others, " they may have been misstatements or fallacies, which cannot be exposed." In some, " there were circumstances of the most atrocious misconduct ; " others " were vaccinations in nothing but the name."

In considering the subject of vaccinal syphilis, it is very necessary " to distinguish between *vaccination properly performed* and the *malapraxis* of an individual vaccinator."

These questions, difficult at present to answer by any sort of deduction from general pathological principles, and surely not empirically answered by the few published cases, in which the vaccinator who has inoculated syphilis declares himself to . have been blameless in the matter, receive, fortunately, a sort of practical answer, and, as regards the probabilities of the case, seem quite overwhelmingly negatived when common experience is appealed to.

If our ordinary current vaccination propagates syphilis, where is the syphilis that it propagates ? Who sees it ? The experience of this department is an entire blank on the subject. For the last ten years we have been in incessant intimate communication with the different parts of England on details of public vaccination, and, during these years, every one of the about 3,500 vaccination districts into which

England is divided, has been visited three or four times by an inspector, specially charged with the duty of minutely investigating the local practice of vaccination ; yet no inspector has ever reported any local accusation or suspicion that a vaccinator had communicated syphilis. Again, our national vaccine establishment has been in existence for more than sixty years, vaccinating at its own stations every year several thousands of applicants, and transmitting to other stations supplies of lymph, with which every year very many other thousands are vaccinated, who, in their turn, become sources of vaccination to others ; but this vast experience does not, so far as I can ascertain, include knowledge of even one solitary case in which it has been alleged that the lymph has communicated syphilis. Is it conceivable that these negative experiences should be adduced, if the vaccine lymph of children with latent hereditary syphilis were an appreciable danger to the public health ?

(Page 46.) Indisputable certainties, which any one can verify for himself, are : First, that year by year millions of vaccinations are performed in Europe with scarcely a solitary accusation transpiring that syphilis has been communicated by any of them ; and, secondly, that physicians and surgeons who could not fail to see such cases in abundance, if such abundance were a reality, concur with almost absolute uniformity in declaring they have never, in all their experience, seen even a single case of the kind. Surely, for every practical purpose, certainties like these are our best guides ; and were such certainties in our knowledge, it would be the merest pedantry to insist on infinitesimal speculative uncertainties, as though our English system of vaccination deserved mistrust, because we are puzzled to explain some alleged syphilizations on the continent.

————o————

[K.]

EDUCATIONAL VACCINE STATISTICS, ENGLAND

[12th Report Medical Officer of the Privy Council, page 48.]

The vaccinator of an Educational Vaccinating Station, during his attendance thereat, will exhibit and explain the course and characters of the vaccine vesicle ; will practically teach the best method or methods of performing vaccination, and of taking lymph for present or future use ; will inculcate all precautions which are necessary with regard to the health of subjects proposed for vaccination, and with regard to the selection and preservation of lymph, and will give all such other instruction as is requisite for the scientific and successful performance of vaccination and re-vaccination. * * * * The Certificate of Proficiency will be understood to imply, and therefore the teacher who signs it will have taken care to ascertain, that the person to whom it is given can skillfully vaccinate, both with liquid lymph (including such as is preserved in capillary tubes,) and also from ivory points ; that he can properly charge ivory points or capillary tubes with lymph ; that he is aware of the relative advantages of recent and preserved lymph, and of all precautions which are requisite in using the latter ; that from among vaccinated subjects presented for eighth-day inspection he can select, and give reasons for preferring, those who are' fittest to furnish lymph ; that, besides being thoroughly familiar with all local changes which, from first to last, normally ensue on vaccination, he has learned what causes may accelerate or retard the local changes, or give them undue severity, or otherwise render them irregular ; that he is well informed as to the constitutional effect of vaccination (including the eruptions which sometimes follow it), and as to the treatment which cases of vaccination, under various circumstances, may require ; that he knows how far the protective influence of vaccination is affected by the lapse of time, and how far by the mode in which it is performed, especially by the number, or size, of vesicles, and knows generally under what circumstances re-vaccination is to be recommended ; finally, that he is acquainted with the laws and regulations relative to public vaccination, and understands the local arrangements which are necessary for maintaining a constant supply of lymph.

--------o--------

[L.]

PROPERLY PERFORMED VACCINATION.

Some of the instructions of the Privy Council of England to its Public Vaccinators. 12th Report, page 49.

1. Except there be immediate danger of small-pox, vaccinate only subjects who are in good health. Satisfy yourself that there is not any eruption behind the ears or elsewhere

on the skin ; nor any febrile state ; nor any irritation of the bowels. Under no circumstances vaccinate a subject to whom, from the state or prospect of his health, vaccination is likely to prove injurious.

6. Consider yourself strictly responsible for the quality of whatever lymph you use or furnish for vaccination. Take lymph only from subjects who are in good health, especially satisfying yourself that they are free from eruption on the skin. Take it only from well-characterized, uninjured vesicles. Do not take it from cases of re-vaccination. Take it (as may be done in all regular cases on the day week after vaccination,) at a time when the vesicles are plump, either just before the formation of the areola, or, at the latest, not more than twenty-four hours after the areola has begun to form.

7. In vaccinating from arm to arm, and still more in proceeding to store lymph, avoid draining any vesicle which you puncture.

8. Scrupulously observe, in your inspection, every sign which tests the efficiency or purity of your lymph. Note any case wherein the vaccine vesicle is unduly hastened, or otherwise irregular in its development, or wherein any undue local irritation arises, and if similar results ensue in other cases vaccinated with the. same lymph, desist at once from employing it.

9. If, from any cause, your supply of lymph ceases, or becomes unsuitable for further use, take immediate measures for obtaining a new supply.

10. Keep in good condition the lancets or other instruments which you use for vaccinating, and do not use them for other surgical operations. Supplies of lymph, guaranteed by the National Vaccine Board, are furnished on application to all medical practitioners.

In the present connection, too, it deserves notice that, among their Lordships' regulations which have been in force for the last ten years, is one requiring the public vaccinator in every case where he vaccinates, to particularize, in a special column of his register, the lymph-source from which the vaccination is done, so that if afterwards, in any case, an accusation against the lymph should arise, the question of fitness or unfitness of the source can at once be properly investigated.

[M.]

CONCLUSIONS OF THE IMPERIAL ACADEMY OF MEDICINE ON ANIMAL AND HUMAN VACCINE.

Page 128 M. Guerin's Discourses.

The Academy, áfter having heard the report of the Commission appointed to experiment with Animal Vaccine, and the discussion which the report has elicited, are of the opinion, that—

1. Animal Vaccine, in its evolution, march and character, presents three grand "analogies," and also some differences with the Human, or Jennerian Vaccine. These analogies do not necessarily imply, on the part of the Animal Vaccine, a prophylactic virtue against small-pox equal to that of the Jennerian. Time and experience can alone definitely settle this question.

2. The Human, or Jennerian Vaccine, whose efficacy and benefit a long and vast experience has established, does not appear susceptible of losing its virtues, but transiently, and in consequence of a want of care in the choice of the vaccinifer, or of the neglect of the rules necessary for a good vaccination. The complications which sometimes alter its purity, but very rarely, can be prevented by greater attention on the part of the vaccinator.

3. Therefore, the Academy declared that the greatest liberty should be given for the demonstration of the propriety and value of Animal Vaccine ; but this liberty must not be exercised at the expense of the Human Vaccine, for the Jennerian Vaccine is entitled to the continued confidence of science and of the public.

————o————

ACKNOWLEDGMENTS.

Besides the distinguished gentlemen who have honored me with the foregoing letters, I am indebted to A. D. Bender, M. D., and B. Illoway, M. D., of Cincinnati, who have kindly aided me in the translation of the German and French letters.

WM. B. DAVIS.

REPORT ON OBITUARIES,

——BY——

B. B. LEONARD, M. D., WEST LIBERTY, OHIO.

OBITUARY NOTICES

—BY—

B. B. LEONARD, M. D., WEST LIBERTY, O.

Time, in its ceaseless flight, has numbered with the irrevocable past, another year, and we are again called upon to pay our tribute of affection and respect to the memory of our professional brethren who have died within the last year. Death, as if in revenge upon a profession which uses its skill and abilities in resisting his attacks and preventing the accomplishment of his designs, has, during the last year or two, visited our Society with a heavy hand, and has taken home, as captives to grace his triumphs, some of our brightest, best, and most successful members. And while we come together to consult upon the most skillful means and about the most successful methods with which to combat this fell destroyer,—who claims the race for his own,—let us turn aside from our business, for a little time, and remember those who have heretofore counseled with us in the unequal struggle.

GEORGE MENDENHALL, M. D.

While the American Medical Association was in session, at Detroit, Michigan, on the 4th day of June, 1874, a distinguished member of this Society,—and one who, on account of his learning and his zeal in the cause of medicine, had formerly been chosen to, and had filled creditably and honorably, the high position of President of that

Association,—yielded his life to that fell destroyer, to the thwarting of whose attacks he had directed his energies, skill and abilities for a period of *forty years.*

Dr. Mendenhall was born in Sharon, Beaver County, Pennsylvania, May 5, 1814. Early in life he exhibited his talents end predilections for the study of medicine, and from his youth up, pursued his studies—as all must who would attain eminent success in the profession—with that entire devotion, unflagging interest and earnestness, which is only prompted by the love of medical science, the hope of advancing and promoting it, and the desire to improve and benefit his fellows. He was fortunate in the choice of a preceptor, having commenced his studies under the late Dr. Benjamin Stanton, of Salem, Ohio. After two and one-half years of dilligent study under so capable an instructor, he entered the University of Pennsylvania, and graduated therefrom in 1835, and before he had attained his majority. Shortly after his graduation he entered upon the practice of his profession, in the city of Cleveland, and through his energy, his industry, and his abilities, soon gained the confidence and esteem of the people of that city, and received a fair share of professional and popular favor and patronage.

In 1837 he removed to Philadelphia, to accept the position of Resident Physician in the Pennsylvania Hospital, but in the spring of the next year returned to Cleveland, in which city he remained—continuing to receive renewed marks of the respect and confidence of the people— until 1843, when, admonished of threatened loss of health, he was forced to seek a more congenial climate, and in that year he moved to Cincinnati; and, undaunted by his impaired health, undismayed by the difficulties that attend the stranger who enters upon the practice in a strange city without influential friends and patrons, and with a dependent family, he entered upon the successful and brilliant career which only terminated with his death. His industrious habits of study, his fidelity to his patients, his thorough qualification for the practice of the profession, in all its branches, and his previous valuable experience, at once secured for him recognition at the hands of his most eminent professional brethren, and his industry and perseverance improved, to the fullest extent, the advantage which he thus early secured. Shortly after his arrival in the city he became associated with Drs. Vattier, and others, in conducting the City Dispensary, and, in company with others, he organized a Summer School of Medicine, which was successfully conducted for a number of years. He was also associated for a considerable time with the late Dr. L. M. Lawson, in editing and publishing the *Western Lancet.*

In addition to the duties and labors consequent upon a large and increasing business, Dr. Mendenhall, with other medical gentlemen of Cincinnati, in 1852, engaged in the organization of the Miami Medical College, which enterprise was crowned with success. In 1869 he was elected President of the American Medical Association. In 1872, on account of failing health, he visited Europe, and in June of that year, was elected a fellow of the Obstetrical Society of London. In 1873 he returned to Cincinnati, where he afterward suffered an attack of paralysis, which eventuated in his death on the 4th of June, 1874.

Dr. Mendenhall gave to the professsion and the world some of the benefits and advantages which he acquired by his earnest study, ripe thought, and active actual experience, and his contributions to medical literature are regarded as good authority and valuable acquisitions upon important subjects. In the death of this member, our Society has lost a wise counsellor, one whose habits of thought and study furnish us an example scarcely to be improved upon, and worthy of careful imitation.

ISAAC W. RUSSELL, M. D.

Died on the 12th day of April, 1876, at Mount Vernon, Ohio. Dr. Russell was the youngest son of the venerable and distinguished Dr. J. W. Russell of that city, long and favorably known to the profession and people of Ohio. He was born in Mount Vernon, where he received his primary education, which was afterward completed at Oberlin. When fully prepared to begin the study of medicine, he entered the office of his father, where he enjoyed rare opportunities for rapid advancement in all that pertained to the study and practice of medicine and surgery. He graduated in the medical department of the University of Michigan, and began practice in his native city. His success and pre-eminence soon brought him conspicuously before the public, and in the organization of the Columbus Medical College, he was chosen adjunct professor of Surgery—a position to which he was peculiarly fitted by dilligent and faithful study. Within the last two years he suffered frequent attacks of pulmonary hemorrhage. His death was sudden, and caused by congestion of the lungs. Alas—Such men die too soon.

————o————

J. W. KINSMAN, M. D.

Dr. Kinsman died on the 18th of July, 1874, at the residence of his son-in-law, Henry Carter, in Lancaster, Ohio. The deceased was born in Ellsworth, Trumbull County, October 18, 1815. When quite young he began the study of medicine, and went to Philadelphia in 1833 and took lectures in the Jefferson Medical College. Returning, he began the practice of medicine in his native town. In 1847 he took the degree of Doctor in Medicine, in the medical college in Cleveland, and removed with his family to Ashland and practiced his profession for two

years, when he left that place and went to the State of
California. After an absence of two years, he returned
and again resumed his practice, which he continued with
the exception of short intervals, until his last illness rendered him unable to perform professional duties.   In the
death of Dr. Kinsman the community lost a good, true
and esteemed citizen—one who commanded the confidence
and respect of all who knew him, and it was justly merited.
He was the father of a large family of children, all of
whom have received a good education, and are occupying
positions of usefulness and responsibility.   From resolutions passed by the Ashland Medical Society, we learn that
he was highly esteemed by his professional brethren. His
age was 58 years.

———o———

A. METZ, M. D.

Dr. Metz was born in Stark County, Ohio, in 1828.   At
a very early age he suffered the loss of his parents, and
was left an orphan without patrimony, but endowed by his
creator with more than ordinary energy and perseverance.
At the age of *twelve years* he had prepared for, and did
teach a district school as a means of support.   Arriving at
the age of sixteen years, he had acquired sufficient preliminary education, to enable him to enter the office of
Dr. Kahler, of Columbiana County, as a student of medicine.   Here he laid broad and deep the foundation for a
position of professional usefulness and distinction, attained
by few.   After taking lectures for one term in Willoughby
Medical College, he enlisted as a soldier during the late
war with Mexico, and was soon detailed as a surgeon.   Not
serving his country with a view to acquire wealth, he returned to his home, poor and unable for a year or so to
resume his studies.   He soon, however, graduated with
honor from the Cleveland Medical College, and began

practice in the county in which he had been a private pupil. He afterwards practiced in Hancock County, and also in Seneca. He settled permanently in Massillon, in 1854. Here his practice increased with his merits, and he added to a general practice, the specialty in which he afterwards became so distinguished—Ophthalmology. In this specialty he acquired such distinction and confidence, and his business so increased, that it compelled the relinquishment of his general practice, all his time being necessary to the fulfillment of his duties as specialist. At the time of his death, he had no less than one hundred and twenty seven patients in the city of Massillon, most of whom were from abroad, seeking relief at his hands. His treatise on Ophthalmology is now regarded as a work of great merit. He occupied the chair of Ophthalmic Surgery in the medical department of the University of Wooster at the time of his death. His life presents an example of industry, perseverance and success, worthy of extensive immitation. His disease was Peritonitis, and proved speedily fatal, February 1, 1876. "Be ye also ready for in such an hour as ye think not, the Son of Man cometh."

————o————

J. H. NAU, M. D.,

Of Carroll, Ohio, died on the 5th of December, 1875, at the age of 29 years. He graduated at the Miami Medical College in the spring of 1872, and at once entered upon the practice of his profession, at Carroll, and by his previous dilligent and continued study, soon won the confidence and respect of the citizens of the village and vicinity. His practice became general and his services highly appreciated. His amiable wife, who was a victim of Phthisic, died in the spring of 1875. This event, together with his arduous labors and mental anxiety, so affected his health that he was advised to take rest and recreation. This he refused to do, as he did not feel willing to desert his post of duty and labor. He felt the responsibility which rests on the truly conscientious prescriber, and met it nobly. He was a sincere Christian, and died in full hope of a glorious immorality. His few short years were sufficient to develope a character of peculiar excellence. He passed away "As sets the morning star which goes not down behind a darkened West, nor hides obscured among the tempests of the sky, but melts away into the light of heaven."

———o———

BENJAMIN STANTON BROWN, M. D.,

Ex-President of the Ohio State Medical Society.

From a communication of Dr. W. D. Scarff, in regard to this man, I learn the following, which is so replete with facts, that I adopt and report it as a fit tribute to his memory:

Dr. Brown was born in Brownsville, Pennsylvania, July 13, 1800, and died in Bellefontaine, Ohio, December 19, 1873. During his early childhood his parents emigrated to Ohio and settled in the neighborhood of Mt. Pleasant, where they remained for a few years, and came to Logan County in the year 1818. At that time the county was almost a wilderness, with few white inhabitants; but numerous bands of Indians roamed through its forests. Notwithstanding these unfavorable surroundings, the young man obtained a very good English education, and before reaching his majority was employed, in the winter season, as a school teacher, but in summer was engaged in agricultural pursuits. When about twenty-one years of age, in consequence of impaired health, he sought a more genial clime in the "sunny regions of the South," and for about three years sojourned in the States of Missis-

sippi and Louisiana, spending most of the time along the
borders of the Gulf of Mexico. After this he returned to
Logan County, and commenced the study of medicine in
the office of the late Dr. Crew, of Zanesfield, and in the
spring of 1828 graduated at the Medical College of Ohio.
In the same year he located in Bellefontaine, where he
continued the practice of medicine for about *thirty-five
years.* "In 1844," Dr. Scarff says, "I made the acquaintance of Dr. Brown, and soon afterwards an intimacy
commenced which continued, uninterruptedly, to the day
of his death. Outside of his own family, none knew him
better than I. He was my rival in business for more than
twenty years, but always an honorable one, and really
seemed more like a partner than a competitor." ·

Dr. Brown was a man of more than ordinary mental
capacity; he was a good physician, of sound judgment, a
safe counsellor, a man of very general intelligence, and, in
or out of the profession, a high-toned and honorable gentleman. Being naturally modest and unassuming, he was
most appreciated by those who knew him best. In 1866
he was elected President of the Ohio State Medical Society, and presided at one of the meetings held at White
Sulphur Springs. The honor could not have been conferred on a more worthy member. About that time he
retired from practice, but continued to take a deep interest
in the profession of his choice, and, so long as his health
permitted, was a regular attendant of the State Society,
and also the American Medical Association, whether at
New Orleans, San Francisco, or the cities of the Eastern
seaboard. Having been reared in the Society of Friends,
he carried with him many of the habits of that exemplary
class of Christians through life. His disease was Haema-
turia, from which he suffered for nearly three months.
His mind was clear and unclouded to the last, and he
waited with Christian patience and resignation for the
approaching change, for he was looking for "a better

country," where death and pain and change shall be no more. His end was peace. He departed as the sun when he sits in his gorgeousness, but leaves the brightness of his reflection above the place of his repose.

————o————

GEORGE A. DEAN, M. D.

Died on the 28th day of February, 1875, at his residence in McComb, Hancock County, Ohio. Aged 53 years. Dr. Dean was born on the 16th day of April, 1822, in Wurtemburg, Germany, and came to the United States at an early age. He received the degree of Doctor in Medicine at the medical department of the Western Reserve College in 1857. His many virtues and excellent character endeared him to the community in which he practiced. In a communication from one of his professional friends, I am assured that "no sculptured marble or granite pile is needed to keep his memory green and fresh in the hearts of those who knew him." "His epitaph is written in the hearts of those, who have received his kindness." "After life's fitful fever, he sleeps well."

————o————

THOMAS S. CLASON, M. D.

Dr. Clason was born in Madisonville, Hamilton County, December 9, 1827. After receiving a preliminary education, he began the study of medicine as a private pupil, and afterwards entered the Medical College of Ohio, and graduated in that institution in March, 1855. He located at Spring Hills, Ohio, where he acquired a good practice, and enjoyed the confidence of the people as a skillful and safe prescriber. When the late war was in progress, and his services were called for, he entered one of the Ohio regiments as an assistant surgeon. He was captured, and held for a while at Richmond, Virginia. On being exchanged, he resigned his commission and settled in Bellefontaine, where he secured a fair practice, and died April 27, 1873.

————o————

ADAM MOSGROVE, M. D.

Died in Urbana, O., March 3, 1875, in the 85th year of his age. Dr. Adam Mosgrove, one of the most highly respected, as well as one of the oldest members of the profession. He was born in County Tyrone, in Ireland, on the 12th day of August, 1790. After receiving a liberal and thorough preparation therefor, he entered upon the regular course of study at the Medical College in Edinburgh, Scotland, from which he entered the Royal College of Surgeons, at Dublin, in Ireland, graduating therefrom. Upon his graduation he was commissioned a surgeon in the British Navy, and in 1816 sailed for America in the ship "Charlotta," of which he was surgeon. On his arrival in the United States he resigned his commission in the Navy, and entered on the practice of his profession in the *New World*, settling first at Lancaster, Pennsylvania, and afterward at Elizabethtown, in the same State. In 1818, with a view to better his condition, and a desire to be with old friends from his native land, he, taking his worldly possessions with him, braved the hardships, exposures and dangers of a lengthy trip across the mountains, and through the then almost unbroken wilderness, and made his weary way to the now city of Urbana, of which place he continued to be a valuable, useful and honored citizen to the day of his death. In common with the other noble pioneers, who, by their virtues, industry, energy and intelligence, laid the broad and deep foundations on which the glorious structure of our State has been reared; he endured the privations, the trials, the discouragements and the difficulties which then surrounded pioneer life, and by his prudence, care, skill and zeal in all the varied relations and trying duties, which attended the practice of medicine at that time, honored the profession, and gained the esteem and respect of all with whom he came in contact. He was possessed of indomitable energy, industry and perseverance, and during the whole course of his professional life, he would permit nothing to come between, or interfere with that full discharge of duty, which he conceived and felt was due to the patient, who had entrusted his life or his health to his care and skill. His constant devotion to his profession, his high toned morality, his sterling integrity and christian character presented an example, worthy of careful imitation. In all the relations of life, whether as physician, citizen, husband, or father, he performed his part well. Like a stock of corn fully ripe, this venerable Nestor of the profession, after more than half a century's arduous and laborious practice, full of years and honors, has been gathered to his fathers. Well might he, conscious of a life well spent in attending to suffering humanity, in ministering to the wants of the maimed and diseased, and both, by precept and example, making the world wiser, better and brighter — like the patriarch, "Gather up his feet into his bed" and depart in peace.

DECEASED PRESIDENTS.

S. M. SMITH, M. D.,

——BY——

THAD. A. REAMY, M. D., CINCINNATI.

DECEASED PRESIDENTS.

S. M. SMITH, M. D.

BY

THAD. A. REAMY, M. D., CINCINNATI.

Dr. Samuel Mitchell Smith, 25th President of the Ohio State Medical Society, was born in Greenfield, Highland county, Ohio, November 28, 1816. He was the only son of Samuel and Nancy Smith—people of intelligence and sterling Christian integrity. These qualities were early planted in the head and heart of the subject of this sketch, and matured in vigor and beauty, bearing rich fruits in abundance throughout his whole life.

Young Smith entered Miami University, at Oxford, O., in the fall of 1832, graduating in 1836. After graduating he engaged for a time in teaching. For two years he had charge of an Academy at Rising Sun, Indiana. During this period he read medicine under the supervision of Dr. Morrison, of Rising Sun, and also attended a course of lectures in Cincinnati. After a second course of lectures in the same institution, he went to Philadelphia, graduating from the University of Pennsylvania. During his pupilage in Philadelphia, he united with the Old School Presbyterian Church, of which he remained a consistent and ardent member to his death. Most of the time during his long residence in Columbus, he was an Elder in the church—to which high office he always contributed the dignity and wisdom of a cultured mind, the benign influence of a spiritually-sanctified heart.

8

Dr. Smith was appointed Assistant Physician to the Central Ohio Lunatic Asylum, entering upon his duties in 1840. The Medical Superintendent was Dr. Wm. Awl. This was his first professional work; he filled this position about three years with zeal and success.

In July, 1843, he entered upon the general practice of his profession, having resigned his position in the Asylum, and opened an office in Columbus. The same year he was married to Miss Susan E. Anthony, of Springfield, O. The now stricken wife survives him.

When Willoughby Medical College was removed to Columbus, Dr. S. was appointed Professor of Materia Medica and Therapeutics; and when Starling Medical College was established, in 1848, its founder and patron, Lyne Starling, appointed Dr. Smith one of the Trustees,—which position he held at the time of his death. He held in this Institution a professorial position, almost constantly, from soon after its organization to the close of his life, filling the chairs of Materia Medica, Theory and Practice of Medicine, &c. He was for many years Dean of the Faculty. He was appointed, by Gov. Chase, a Trustee of the Central Ohio Lunatic Asylum, which position he filled for eighteen years, most of the time acting as President of the Board. At the beginning of the war Dr. Smith was appointed, and served, on the Board of Examiners of Army Surgeons. Many of us remember him in that position. To it he brought the thoroughness of his broad professional culture, the courteousness and fairness of the high-toned gentleman. He had charge of several expeditions to bring wounded and sick soldiers to Ohio, rendering signal service. He was appointed on the staff of Gov. Todd, as Surgeon-General of Ohio. In this capacity his duties were onerous: equipping and sending Surgeons to the field. He was for many years Physician to the Asylum for the Deaf and Dumb, located at Columbus. He was a prominent and active delegate to the Prison Reform Congress, held in Europe in 1872.

Dr. Smith possessed, in an eminent degree, the highest qualifications for a physician, being endowed with a vigorous physical and mental organization; possessed of untiring industry and energy ; receiving in early life a thorough classical education, which was broadened and deepened in maturity of manhood; studying and practicing his profession with enthusiasm ; devoting himself to its duties with a sacrificing spirit which never consulted his own ease or comfort, but always the welfare of his patients. He had courage of the highest type, but a heart as tender as that of a little child. To the sick-room he carried the judgment and intelligence of thorough and constant medical study,—always being fully up in the very latest medical literature, the good of which he was able to cull with rare skill and wisdom. With his patients he was tender and always in full sympathy—genial and hopeful in disposition, pure and spotless in his life, he came into the presence of the afflicted truly as "the good physician." In diagnosis he was clear, systematic and accurate, prescribing with promptness and skill. As a teacher, he was painstaking, conscientious and practical, conservative and sound. In professional intercourse, he was honorable to the fullest degree. As a citizen, he was intelligent, liberal and of faultless reputation. As a husband and father, he was just, generous and indulgent. A man, great in goodness and usefulness has fallen, but the works of his life they do live, and his crown and glory are immortal.

Dr. S. M. Smith died in Columbus, O., Nov. 30, 1874, aged 58 years. The subjoined is the result of the *post mortem* examination.*

AUTOPSY OF DR. S. M. SMITH.

December 1st, 1874, twenty-four hours after death.

Aged 58. Body emaciated ; scalp and bones of the cranium healthy and normal. Dura mater in many places adherent

*The writer is indebted to the Columbus Press for much of the information contained in this obituary notice, but an intimate acquaintance of twenty-five years places him in position to fully appreciate its truth. Prof. Smith was one of the writer's first medical teachers.

to the arachnoid, which latter was abnormally opaque and thickened where free. Optic nerves equally well developed and normal. Ophthalmic and vertebral arteries, athero-matous, cylindrical and patulous. Basilar artery and carotids with their branches, with small atheromatous patches, and partly filled with blood. The substance of the cerebral hemis-pheres presented a dull, darkened appearance, (light brownish,) probably due to capillary conjestion. The lateral ventricles were distended with a turbid serum of a brownish tinge. The choroid plexus brownish and soggy. The third (3rd) ventricle was empty, but appeared to have been in the same condition as the lateral, the serum having probably escaped by the torn infundibulum or the cut medulla oblongata. The middle commissure of this ventricle was broken down and entirely obliterated. The fifth (5th) ventricle was largely distended with nearly transparent serum. The optic thal-amus, corpus callosum and pons Varolii presented the same darkened appearance as the cerebrum. The fornix, anterior and posterior commissures of third ventricle, normal, or nearly so. Corpora quadrigemina and pineal gland small, apparently from pressure.

The inferior surface of the cerebellum presented elevated rough deposits attached to the dura mater, resembling tubercu-lar deposits. Section of the cerebellum presented a semi-transparent, yellowish, waxy appearance throughout, and when subjected to a stream of water, immediately became flocculent and broken up.

No other organs were examined. No indication of cere-bral hemorrhage existed.

Post Mortem made by Drs. Wheaton and Halderman.

ON

ESMARCH'S BANDAGE IN MINOR SURGERY,

——BY——

J. H. POOLEY, M. D.,

Professor of Surgery in Starling Medical College,

COLUMBUS, OHIO.

ON ESMARCH'S BANDAGE IN MINOR SURGERY.

—BY—

J. H. POOLEY, M. D.,

Professor of Surgery in Starling Medical College,

COLUMBUS, OHIO.

The fact that some of the largest operations in surgery, and those unavoidably accompanied hitherto by considerable loss of blood, could be accomplished without any bleeding at all, when first announced by the distinguished Professor of Kiel, struck the surgical world with admiration and astonishment. The simplicity of the means by which this wonderful result was obtained, was as remarkable as the result itself. Everybody hastened to verify the procedure,—which in no case met with absolute disappointment,—and in an exceedingly short space of, time it took its place among the most valuable acquisitions of modern surgery, and was all but universally adopted. While all admitted its value, some envious souls were found to dispute its novelty and originality. They tried to show that there was nothing new in it, because, for a very long time surgeons had endeavored to diminish the loss of blood in amputations, by previously bandaging as well as elevating the limb. But they have failed altogether to show that any such practice was ever generally or extensively adopted, or that it ever produced anything like a perfect result.

The fact is, that the principle of *elastic* pressure, applied in Esmarch's manner, is as absolutely new, as much of an original improvement, as were anæsthetics themselves. No one seeks to invalidate the claims of modern anæsthesia; because, in the oldest books on medicine we find formulæ more or less ineffective to abrogate or lessen the pain of surgical operations, neither should we withhold our eulogies here because surgeons in all ages, and by multifarious expedients, have endeavored to prevent the loss of blood. Both desiderata were of course as old as surgery itself, and both remained practically unsolved until in our day, thanks to Simpson and Morton and Esmarch, we witness the wonderful spectacle of limbs removed, and other serious operations performed, without pain and without bleeding. So much has been said, written, and printed upon this subject, that I fear many will think that anything further on it is superfluous, if not impertinent. I cannot think so, however, as long as I occasionally witness, and hear of, as I have done since coming to the West, of amputations performed with the old method, and with copious hemorrhage, in patients already largely depleted by blood-loss following serious accidents, just as if Esmarch's method had never been invented, or, was almost unknown. I have used it, I suppose, in over a hundred operations of varying magnitude and severity, and only once have I had reason to think that it was accompanied with the slightest drawback. In that case,—a somewhat protracted operation upon the foot in an aged man,—gangrene followed; it may have been in part from the elastic bandage, it may have been altogether from the patient's advanced age and unfavorable condition; I cannot tell. But at any rate, all that can be legitimately deduced from that one unfavorable circumstance is, that care needs to be exercised in the tightness of the bandage and the length of time it is left applied upon the extremities of old and feeble persons. And it is by the accumulation of just such experiences that we have to learn to use properly all the potent agencies of medicine and surgery.

Whatever is capable of positive and great good, is of course also capable of doing harm; if this were not so, very little skill, learning, or judgment, would be needed to make a successful practitioner, but the merest routinest would do as well.

But this paper was not undertaken to advocate the use of Esmarch's bandage as a blood saving agent in capital operations,—that is hardly necessary,—but rather to point out and emphasize its convenience and utility in those smaller operations, that are known as Minor Surgery, performed every day by the general practitioner, and often done in the physician's office.

Nothing could exceed my delight, and sense of new power, when I first amputated the thigh without seeing a single drop of blood till after the operation was finished and all the principal and some of the smaller arteries secured. I realized at once that a great step had been taken, not only in saving blood to the patient, but in the convenience of the surgeon,—in the quietness and precision with which every step could be performed,—and in the independence of assistants that was acquired. Of course, at first there was something of the uncertainty and lack of perfect security of feeling that always attends the use of a new proceedure under such circumstances,—just such a feeling as kept you awake all night, perhaps, the first time you used acupressure, half fearing to be suddenly called and told your patient was bleeding to death. But very soon this gave way to absolute confidence; and now, with Esmarch's bandage, I should think nothing of amputating without any assistant, except one to administer the ether.

In these more considerable operations, however, there is almost always abundance of assistance on hand, or abundance of time to summon it, while in minor matters one either has not time to send for help, or deems the occasion too insignificant, and yet finds the fact of hemorrhage the most annoying source of imperfection and delay in what promised to be an easy or trifling operation. In such little matters as the removal of needles or other foreign bodies, the amputation of fingers or toes, the exsection of the smaller joints, the removal of dead bone, small tumors, excision of nerves, &c., &c., or in the dressing of wounds, the bloodless method is beyond all praise. Of course there is no question here, unless, perhaps, in a few of the most exceptional cases, of saving blood for the patient's sake. But to have the incisions perfectly clean and dry, to see every tissue as you divide it, to have no spattering or soiling of office carpet or furniture, to be able to finish your operation quietly and at ease and send your patient home with his dressing and bandage nicely adjusted,—often without even a stain of blood upon it,— makes operating a pleasure and a luxury, and will enable us to do many things in ordinary office practice that otherwise would have to be postponed, and to do them a great deal better and more neatly, too.

Permit me, in illustration of the utility of Esmarch's bandage—in what I may call office surgery, to relate a few cases :

Case 1.—Mr. C., a gentleman between 40 and 50 years of age, consulted me for a very severe and persistent digital neuralgia, affecting the second, or middle finger of the right hand. This affection had come on several years previously, without any known cause, and had been increasing in severity ever since. The pain was not constant, but paroxysmal, the paroxysms at times being exceedingly severe, almost unbearable, they were of various duration, from a few minutes to many hours, confined almost exclusively to the affected finger and most severe around the matrix of the nail, but occasionally shooting up the forearm. A paroxysm would always be excited by a blow, or pressure, or any contact beyond the very slightest on the pulp of the finger, so that he lived in constant dread of such an occurrence, and hardly had a care beyond the protection of the sensitive digit. He had been subjected to a great variety of treatment, including various narcotics and sedatives, both generally and locally, electricity, etc., and on one occasion had a lunated incision corresponding to the outline of the matrix made down to the bone, and kept open some time before being allowed to heal. These means were all alike unavailing. A careful examination failed to find any derangement of his general health, or any local condition, or anything in his habits or antecedents to account for his neuralgia. I suggested to him as the only means I thought likely to benefit him, the exsection of a portion of the digital nerve on each side of the finger. He readily gave his assent. I applied the principal of Esmarch's bandage in the following way: A strip of india rubber about an inch wide and six inches long, procured by dividing at one point one of the broad rubber rings used to keep together packages of paper, &c. constituted the bandage, and one of the thick round india rubber rings sometimes used round the ends of the ribs of an umbrella, the torniquet, applied at the base of the finger. This extemporized apparatus, proved both convenient and perfectly efficient. A lateral incision extending the length of the internode, between the first and second phalangeal articulations, was made on either side of the finger. The nerves were found considerably enlarged. On one side there was a small fusiform swelling in the middle of the exposed portion of the nerve, and on the other two gemmiform, or budlike projections from the nerve. About an inch of the nerve on each side was removed, the sections being made through apparently healthy nerve except that it was enlarged. Not a drop of blood was seen during the operation, the wounds were brought together, and dressed with small strips of isinglass plaster, and covered with colodion, which was allowed to harden before the ring at the base of the finger was removed The wounds healed by first intention, and there has been no return of the neuralgia, although nearly a year has elapsed since the operation. The only resulting inconvenience is partial anæsthesia of the finger.

This case is of itself an exceedingly interesting one, the presence of these neuromata on the nerves of one finger without any evidence of similar growths elsewhere, the resulting neuralgia, and its permanent relief by neurotomy or exsection of the nerves, are all deserving of note. But I report it to show the wonderful convenience of the bloodless method in such delicate little procedures, and the wide field of usefulness thus pertaining to a method, not yet I think fully appreciated except in capital operations. There is an operation now coming into vogue, for the cure of that distortion of the toes known as hallux valgus, or abduction of the great toe, consisting in the removal of the capitulum metatarsi of the distorted joint. This operation, which is abundantly worthy of our confidence, and far superior to all mechanical appliances in these cases, is not altogether easy of execution without the bloodless method, but with it, when all the tissues can be plainly seen, can be handsomely done with complete preservation of the periosteum. In these operations upon the toes, all the toes are included in a broad bandage, it not being feasible to envelope a single toe, as in the case of a finger, but this makes no manner of difference; the same method is adopted when the base of the finger is to be operated upon.

Case 2.—H. B., aged 4 years, had an exostosis growing from the upper surface of the ungual phalanx of the great toe of the right foot, it was exquisitely tender, though not otherwise painful, and would not tolerate the pressure of a shoe. It had by pressure caused the destruction of most of the nail, and was attached by a very broad base. I etherized the little patient, and after applying Esmarch's bandage, proceeded to enucleate the bone at the end of the toe, as I found it impracticable to remove the exostosis in any other way. This was done by making a very short incision along the dossum of the toe, starting from the upper convex border of the matrix, and then by following the outline of the nail accurately, the bone was exsected, or more properly speaking, enucleated subperiostically, without interfering with the attachment of the flexor or extensor tendon. The wound healed favorably, and now the child wears a shoe, runs, plays and jumps freely, and has perfect flexion and extension of the toe end. I do not say this operation could not have been done without the Esmarch's bandage; but it could not have been done with the same certainty and nicety. It was done in my office; there was no sponging needed, the bandage, put on quite tightly at first, was applied before the tourniquet or rubber tubing was removed, and all was perfectly clean and dry. Everybody knows how annoying, far beyond more serious operations, the attempt to remove broken fragments of needle from the hand or other part is. This arises principally from the constant welling up of the blood in the little space where we are exploring for the foreign body. No sooner is the blood sponged away there, before the forceps or probe can be taken in hand, or the eye survey the spot, it is full of blood again, obscuring everything. Esmarch's bandage obviates all this, and enables us to see just what we are about.

Case 3.—Mr. S., aged 65 years, had a large epithelioma, situated over the external surface of the lower end of the right femur. He had had chronic ulceration here for years, probably connected with some bone disease; it had healed up for some time, leaving the indurated, discolored surface—common after such ulcerations—and from this unhealthy, or devitalized dermoid tissue the epithelioma had grown. It was oval in shape, four inches in length by three in breadth, and projected from the surrounding surface about one inch. The discharge from it was rather profuse and very offensive. Esmarch's bandage was applied, as if for amputation of the thigh, and the growth removed by simply circumscribing it with the knife and dissecting it out. The advantage of the bloodless method was strikingly shown when we came to dig down between the outer hamstring tendon and the bone for the disease, which here penetrated very deeply, and would have been difficult of detection if bleeding had been going on at the time.

Case 4.—J. W., aged 40 years, had in the palm of his right hand a deep cut, eroding ulcer,—probably epitheliomatous,—which had existed two years and resisted every mode of treatment. I applied Esmarch's bandage and removed it thoroughly without a drop of blood making its appearance. The wound healed promptly and the man is well.

To these two last patients no anæsthetic was administered, and though the point is difficult, if not impossible, of absolute and definite determination, I am inclined to think that the bandage produced some degree of local anæsthesia; at any rate, they made very much less complaint of pain than might naturally have been expected. But be this as it may, they certainly derived no inconsiderable advantage from the elastic bandage, from the greater celerity with which it permitted the operation to be performed. It seems to me that these cases, which might be indefinitely multiplied, show plainly that in Esmarch's bandage the surgeon has a means at hand of facilitating minor operations, and promoting his own confidence and comfort, which is worth fully as much as an assistant would be, and which deserves to be more fully appreciated. Had Esmarch, by his new method, done no more for us than this, he would deserve out everlasting gratitude.

I anticipate for this method great usefulness in a more serious class of cases, viz: in traumatic aneurism of the extremities, where it will greatly facilitate the performance of the old operation of laying open the sac, turning out the contents and ligaturing the artery above and below the opening in its coats,—an operation which is founded upon a truly philosophical basis, and the great objection to which has been the difficulties attending its performance.

Besides all these applications to *operative* surgery, it seems probable that this procedure may have other triumphs in store. My friend, Dr. Turney, of Circleville, in a paper in the June number of the *Ohio Medical and Surgical Journal,* has called attention to it as an efficacious means of treatment in chronic ulcers; and I can, to a great extent, endorse and corroborate his statement, though I have not made as thorough trial of it as I desire and intend to do.

In varicose veins it deserves a thorough and extended trial, and in elephantiasis of the extremities—so rebellious to other treatment, even to ligature of the main artery— it should be perseveringly tried. It is a simple principle, but a great power, and we have much yet to learn of its application.

There is nothing original or extraordinary in this short paper, but I believe if it leads to a more common use of the elastic bandage in Minor Surgery, and to a careful trial of it in its many uses, it may be productive of a great deal of good.

————o————

DISCUSSION ON DR. POOLEY'S PAPER.

Dr. Hamilton said: "What is Esmarch's Bandage? It is but elastic pressure." He believes in it; but it has its abuses as well as its uses. "To make an operation where not a *drop* of blood is lost, as was stated in the paper last evening, the tissues *must* be compressed to that degree that there is danger of Phlebitis, Cellulitis, Erysipelas, Gangrene, and Sloughing." He could not associate it, with any such brilliant practice as not to lose a drop of blood in an operation. If he had made such brilliant operations with its use, where not even a *drop* of blood was lost, his hair would stand on end at such results. "To strangulate a limb for twenty, thirty, forty or fifty minutes, —an arm, for instance,—is no trifling matter, and not to be flippantly recommended,—the arm, perhaps, that feeds a family of children. I say it has its dangers, and no such pressure can be made without endangering the limb. And all of this for the glory of operating without the loss of a drop of blood, and of preserving immaculate the shirt-bosom and prevent the soiling of a Brussell's carpet. This jugulating a limb for an indefinite time is a serious matter, and should not be, as we have remarked, flippantly recommended."

Dr. Scott said: "There are some conditions where the loss of blood is of advantage. In injuries where there is inflammation and exudation, it is better to cut through them and let the exudation escape, than to compress it and leave it to slough out. In cases of old sequestra the bandage is a good thing; it is a nice thing to have a clean, bloodless surface to work upon. But, with its use, some-times, there will be loss of blood after the circu-lation returns." He liked the paper and believes in the bandage. The paper was short and to the point, and all the better on that account.

Dr. Pooley, in reply, said: "It does not take such force as the gentleman who first spoke seems to imagine, to apply the bandage in such a way as to produce its full effect. Complete bloodlessness is secured with much less than one's full strength in the application. Such a mode of application is entirely unnecessary, and may be injuri-ous. This is the error we are all liable to fall into when first making use of the bandage, and it is only by actual experience that we learn to trust those less forcible applications of it, that are equally efficacious.

"With regard to the evils enumerated as likely to follow the use of the bandage, viz: Phlebitis, Cellulitis, Erysipelas, &c., all there is to say is, that notwithstanding any reasoning or anticipations on the subject, they have not, as a matter of fact, been found to ensue any more frequently, indeed not as frequently, as in operations performed in the ordinary way. To find fault with the bandage because they have sometimes occurred after its use, is no argument; for they occur—alas! but tóo frequently—after operations performed in every way and with every precaution. Some bad consequences seem to have followed the use of this appliance, that may fairly be attributed to its use; but they were in such extremely few instances as to form no argument whatever against it. The principle that would condemn the general use of Esmarch's Bandage on account of such rare and infrequent accidents, would, if carried out, paralize all human effort, and disarm surgery and medicine of every useful appliance against disease and death. The consequences to which I allude are Gangrene and Paralysis. The first occurred to me in one instance; but inasmuch as the patient was old, and had been long intemperate, and the operation was a protracted one upon the foot, it is quite possible the bandage had nothing at all to do with it. This is the only case I have seen reported. There has also been one case reported of *temporary* paralysis following the method, caused, no doubt, by the use of the solid rubber cord as a tourniquet above the bandage,—which is now discarded by all surgeons, and a flat or hollow band used in its stead, from which no such accident has occurred or is likely to occur.

"The gentleman has expressed great horror at the idea of jugulating the limb, as he calls it, for a length of time. I

9

certainly have never seen the bandage kept on for more than half an hour or so at a time; but Langenbeck and others of equal authority, assure us that they have repeatedly kept it on for two hours and a half, with perfect safety. As to the convenience of the operator,—though this is an important matter,—it is of course only of secondary importance, and not to be thought of if it conflicts with the welfare of the patient. But if Langenbeck and others keep the bandage applied for hours, without detriment, surely we are justifiable in applying it for a few minutes, if only for the ignoble purpose of saving our beautiful Brussels carpets, or preserving immaculate the purity of our shirt-bosoms.

THE FORCEPS IN BREECH. DELIVERIES,

—WITH A—

DESCRIPTION OF· A NEW INSTRUMENT,

—BY—

A. J. MILES, M. D.,

Professor of Diseases of Women and Children in the Cincinnati College of Medicine and Surgery; Fellow of the Obstetrical Society of London.

THE FORCEPS IN BREECH DELIVERIES,

WITH A DESCRIPTION OF A NEW INSTRUMENT.

——BY——

A. J. MILES, M. D.

Professor of Diseases of Women and Children in the Cincinnati College
of Medicine and Surgery ; Fellow of the Obstetrical
Society of London.

Leishman in his late work on Obstetrics, gives the proportion of breech presentations, as 1 in 45 mature births.
Of these the mortality has been variously estimated.

In cases born without any interference from the accou-
cheur, 1 in 8 are born dead; in those where artificial
delivery is required, 1 in 3½ cases are born dead.

These figures give the mortality as low as any of our
most sanguine obstetrical writers.

It will be useful in this connection, for us to consider
some of the causes which bring about this fatality in breech
cases.

1st. The breech as a dilating power, is far inferior to
the head. The bag of waters in breech cases does comparatively little in dilating the os; with the os partially
dilated, the membranes ruptured, the breech comes to
exert a pressure on the os. The soft tissues which com-
pose it, its smaller size, as compared with the head, all add
to its disadvantages. With the parturient canal insufficient-
ly open the trunk engages. There is exerted an unusual
pressure on the viscera contained in the abdominal and

thoracic cavities. Death to the child may ensue from this direct pressure compromising the action of the heart. After the trunk the head descends. The descent of the body has already caused such a position of the umbilical cord, that it is subject to pressure between the child and the pelvis. When the head comes down, the traction on the cord is increased and the placenta is torn from its attachments at a time when it is not as yet possible for the child to respire. Here rises a great difficulty. In vertex presentations, the head, the largest part of the fœtus precedes. The parturient canal is dilated to its widest extent by the passage of the head, and the passage of the body is usually a matter of slight difficulty. The contrary is the case in presentation of the breech. Here the smallest part of the fœtus precedes. Now at a time when the maternal circulation can no longer support the life of the child, the head is delayed, by reason of its size, until such time, as it can, by its own power dilate the passage. Suppose the placenta to be still attached while the head is in utero, what is the condition of things? The uterus has expelled the major part of its contents. The head only remains. The uterus relieved of the counter pressure, caused by the presence of the fœtus in its cavity, contracts down to such a degree that placental circulation is impossible.

In the olden times it was thought that the only safe way by which a child could be born, was by presentation of the head. This idea was long since exploded. Instruments were devised and manual methods recommended, by which the fœtus could be delivered in breech cases, even in cases where there was considerable difficulty.

Let us notice for a moment some of the means which are at present used. First, we have the Blunt Hook. This instrument is applied in the flexure of the groin. If there be any resistance of consequence to the passage of the child, one of two things will follow traction made by means of this instrument, viz: the femur will be fractured, or there will be such laceration of the parts, that the future prospects of the child may be endangered thereby. This may occur in several ways,—a laceration in this part is constantly irritated by the passage of the urine, and a very extensive ulceration may take place. If this is not the case, the contusion of the parts may result in abscess or gangrene. Any of these conditions place the child in considerable hazard. I think the experience of all my professional brethren will bear me out, when I say that in cases where the blunt hook is applied, there are bad consequences if any force at all is used, and in such cases where the instrument is applied and where no untoward results have followed, the traction was so slight that the finger would have accomplished the same end, thus making the instrument practically useless.

What is said of the blunt hook is true of the fillet. This apparently harmless instrument is capable of doing a very great amount of damage, and added to this, there is the difficulty of its application. The finger is the best instrument we have in obstetric practice, but there are times when the finger cannot serve our purpose. Suppose we have a case where the breech has descended low in the cavity of the pelvis. From uterine inertia or other causes there is no progress in the case,—we hook our finger into the groin,—we try to move the breech, wedged and immovable,—we fail,—what is to be done? We fear to use the blunt hook or fillet, for experience has taught us the bad results which are liable to follow their use. In such cases the forceps has been recommended by high authority.

There have been many objections urged to the use of the forceps in breech cases.

1st. It has been said that the instrument is liable to slip. This is no more the case than where the instrument is used on the head.

2d. It has been said that the blades of the forceps passing over the ilia would exert undue pressure on the

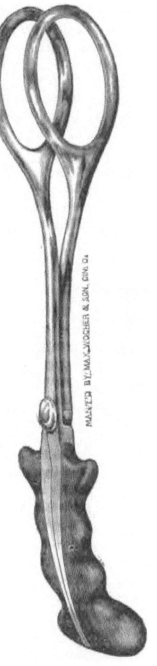

The accompanying cut shows the
side view of the instrument, half
size, and also a front view of the
blades closed, half size.

abdomen of the child.   The bowels will be moved aside
by the presence of the instrument, the only bad consequence is perhaps a slight bluish mark on the abdominal
walls.   How much more severe are frequently the effects
of this instrument when applied to the head.   This has
been the experience of Professor Hueter of Marburg, who
has used the instrument in a large number of cases.

If there be any ground for the above objections, it is, I
think, entirely obviated by the forceps I have devised
especially for use on the breech.   This breech forceps, by
its adaptation to the anatomical construction of the pelvis
of the child, will not, when properly adjusted, slip, or produce undue pressure on the abdomen of the child.   The
length of the entire instrument is 12½ inches; length of
blades, 7½ inches; length of the handle, 5 inches; width
of blades in the widest part, 1¾ inches; length of fenestra,
2⅝ inches; width of fenestra in its widest part, 1¼ inches;
distance of the blades at the widest part, when locked,
2⅛ inches; distance of the tip of the blades when locked,
1¼ inches; length of the expanded part of the blades,
4½ inches.   The advantage of this instrument over the
head forceps for breech cases is apparent, being constructed,
as it is, to fit over the pelvis; spoon-shaped, so as to dip
over the crests of the ilia embracing the trochanters in
the fenestra.   Closely fitting over the pelvis, it affords us all
the power required for extracting the child, and by its
compactness and adaptation to the breech, it is less liable to
injure either the mother or the child than any other instrument previously in use.

The application of the forceps in breech cases is as follows:—In the first position, in which the breech lies in the
left oblique diameter, left trochanter forward, the instrument is adjusted in the following manner: The left blade
is passed in front of the left sacro-iliac-synchondrosis and
is made to take its position over the right trochanter.   The
right blade is passed forward over the left trochanter.   In

the second position, in which the child lies in the right oblique diameter, right trochanter forward, the left blade is passed forward over the right trochanter, the right blade is passed backward in front of the right sacro-iliac-syn-chondrosis over the left trochanter.   Professor Hueter insists that the trochanters should be engaged in the fenestra, and that the ends of the blades project well upon the pelvis of the child.   Should the blades grasp the upper portions of the thighs, the limbs of the child might be injured in extraction.   It would be well during delivery, to examine from time to time the position of the forceps during the intervals between the pains, to see if they remain properly adjusted.   During the extraction of the child, care should be taken to humor the natural movements of rotation, &c.   The forceps should not be removed until the trochanters are born.

Stenosis of the Larynx,

—BY—

BERNARD TAUBER, M. D.,

Lecturer on Laryngoscopy and Diseases of the Throat and Air Passages,

Miami Medical College,

CINCINNATI, OHIO.

STENOSIS OF THE LARYNX.

—BY—

BERNARD TAUBER, M. D.,

Lecturer on Laryngoscopy and Diseases of the Throat and Air Passages,

Miami Medical College, Cincinnati, O.

Under Stenosis of the Larynx are understood not alone those cases in which the cavity of the larynx is so contracted that respiration can only be performed with great difficulty, and then only imperfectly, but also such cases in which, although there be a diminution of the calibre, the respiratory process is not essentially interfered with.

Clinically, Stenosis of the Larynx may be divided into three groups, according to the section of the cavity that be the seat of the trouble: In the section above the glottis, in the glottis itself, or below the glottis.

A.—Narrowing of the section above the Glottis.—Under this head come all cases in which the upper portion of the laryngeal cavity is diminished in size by tumors, or swellings, occupying the interior of that section. In this group may also be classed Oedema of the Ary-epiglottic Folds, and also those cases of narrowing from tumors originating in the pharynx.

B.—Contraction of the Glottis—Stenosis of the Glottis.— This form of stenosis results—

1st. From catarrhal inflammation,—from acute catarrhal inflammation,—producing tumefaction of the true vocal chords, the protrusion of the tumefied false vocal chords into the glottis, swelling of the posterior wall of the larynx, and also difficult upward movement of the vocal chords.

The obstacles to this upward movement are the tumefaction of the vocal chords, as also that of the parts lying from without inwards—especially the false vocal chords—and further swelling of the parts lying outwardly and posteriorly of the arytenoid cartilages, through which the movements of the processus vocales and musculares of the arytenoid cartilages are mechanically impeded. Lastly, we would call attention to the possibility of disturbed muscular action, the cause of which must be sought for either in a spasm of the muscles closing the glottis, or in a paresis of the muscles opening the glottis,—processes occurring also in other forms of inflammation of the laryngeal mucous membrane. *Chronic Catarrhal inflammation* may produce slight narrowing of the glottis from tumefaction of the true vocal chords and the posterior laryngeal wall.

2nd. Syphilitic inflammation of the laryngeal mucous membrane, leads frequently to a greater or less degree of stenosis of the larynx, more particularly of the glottis.

3rd. Croupous inflammation, through the exudated false membrane, causes a narrowing of the glottis. Furthermore, I would call your attention to a more important factor in the production of this trouble, namely, œdema of the vocal chords, which has been observed in croupous inflammation not alone of the parts directly concerned, but also of more distant regions of the larynx, as for instance, the epiglottis, as frequently met with in variola, and which generally proves fatal.

4th. From inflammation and œdema of the vocal chords, and of the upper section of the posterior laryngeal wall from perichondritis laryngea. In cases of perichondritis, sequelæ of typhus, or small-pox and syphilitic perichondritis, the inflammation and œdematous tumefaction of the vocal chords—with or without a similar state of things of the false vocal chords—are no doubt the main factors in the production of the high degree of laryngeal stenosis generally found.

5th. From ulcerations of the true vocal chords. Where these are large, and especially if they occupy the glottis through its whole length, suppuration of the vocal chords has generally already ensued. The stenosis in these cases is caused chiefly by the inflammation and engorgement of the surrounding parts,—more especially of the upper portion of the posterior wall of the larynx. The contraction of the glottis thus resulting may reach a high degree, so great, in fact, that it may become necessary to resort to tracheotomy. In this category belong:

(*a.*) *Syphilitic ulcerations.*

(*b.*) *Diptheritic ulcerations in typhus.*

(*c.*) *Ulcerations coming on in the course of phthisis pulmonalis.*

(*d.*) *Ulcerations of doubtful character that cannot be more particularly described.*

6th. From cicatrices resulting from wounds or ulcerations.

7th. From excrescences: (*a.*) Small papillary growths and other excrescences, though they be situated on the free edges of the true vocal chords, do not very materially narrow the glottis. (*b.*) Syphilitic excrescences. (*c.*) Lupous neoplasms.

8th. From curving or arching of one true vocal chord into the median line, or even beyond this: (*a.*) Through undermining abscesses. (*b.*) From cancer. (*c.*) Abnormal muscular action, causing unilateral stenosis.

C.—Stenosis of that section of the Larynx below the Glottis. —The morbid conditions coming under this head are the following:

1st. A ring-like contraction below the glottis, in which the laryngoscopical examination reveals a round, ring-like border, a little below the true vocal chords, by which the lumen of the larynx is diminished in a greater or lesser degree.

2nd. Perichondritis laryngea.

In this category belong certain cases of this disease, in which the consecutive inflammation and engorgement of the true vocal chords are insufficient to explain, satisfactorily, the very great disturbance of the respiratory process. A stenosis, also, of the section of the larynx below the glottis must, therefore, be assumed.

In stenosis of the larynx above and in the glottis by the direct local operative procedure, the difficulty may be removed, and, in many cases, laryngotomy avoided

For this purpose Prof. Schroetter, of Vienna, has devised a set of hard rubber bougies, ten inches long and of six different sizes in diameter—from ¼ to ¾ inches. These, directed by means of the laryngoscope, are introduced into the larynx once or twice daily, and allowed to remain there from 20 to 30 minutes. This procedure is continued until size No. 6 can be easily introduced. The modus operandi of this procedure is "Dilatation." Whilst in attendance on the Vienna Throat Clinic, I had opportunity to see successful results from this course in syphilitic patients; have there myself introduced the dilators, and after a few weeks the difficulty was removed. I will add that these patients were at the same time put on proper anti-syphilitic treatment.

In narrowing of the glottis and of that portion of the larynx below the glottis, laryngotomy, or tracheotomy, is the operation generally resorted to. If, however, the point of contraction be low down, we will accomplish nothing by the operation.

Stenosis of the larynx, resulting from syphilitic cicatrices or from the swollen condition of the walls of that organ, frequently persists—although an operation has been resorted to—and will not yield.

How can we remedy this evil? To accomplish this object, Prof. Schroetter has also constructed a set of zinc cylinders, 1¾ inches long and of enlarging diameter from ¼ to ¾ inches. Through this cylinder passes a small brass rod, projecting at both ends about one-fourth of an inch, ending at its lower extremity in a button, and having at the upper end an eye, through which a thread from 18 to 20 inches long is drawn. To introduce this bougie into the cavity of the larynx, the thread, by means of a hook-shaped mandrin, is drawn through a canula, with handle attachment. The cylinder having a circular depression at its upper end, fits closely over the canula. The cord is now drawn tight and wound firmly around at the end of the handle, and bougie and canula have become one— forming one instrument 14 inches in length. The cylinder is now oiled, and, with the aid of the laryngoscope, it is now introduced into the larynx, and when properly adjusted the button above mentioned protrudes at the external opening; it is grasped by a pair of pincers—these are fastened by a screw, and the cylinder is firmly fixed and can not be moved up or down. The cord is now loosened at the handle and the canula withdrawn, leaving the cylinder in the larynx. The cord protrudes through the mouth of the patient, without incommoding him whatever in mastication or deglutition. Every twenty-four hours the bougie is withdrawn and again introduced, gradually increasing the size. The modus operandi is here the same—the bougie, by its weight and constant contact, dilating the constricted portion.

This very excellent and most ingenious procedure was first employed in the Vienna Throat Clinic of 1874-5, with most happy results. Its value entitles it to a prominent place in the history of laryngoscopy.

268 ELM STREET.

EXTERNAL USE OF·GLYCERINE

—IN—

CHRONIC HYDROCEPHALUS,

—BY—

A. N. READ, M. D., NORWALK, OHIO.

EXTERNAL USE OF GLYCERINE

— IN —

CHRONIC HYDROCEPHALUS,

— BY —

A. N. READ, M. D.

NORWALK, O.

Case 1.—Child 18 months old; bowels tumid; general emaciation; head measured 24 inches in circumference; sutures separated and bulging of the integuments over the sutures.

Gave a cathartic; then ordered an application made to the head, of Glycerine, with a little Tincture of Iodine, to be applied freely twice a day, and the patient to wear a close-fitting muslin cap. The mother informed me "that the medicine she applied to the head, caused the child to sweat dreadfully." This suggested to me the possibility, that the glycerine, with its strong affinity for water, had caused an exudation of serum, which, if continued, might cure the child. I was strengthened in the hope of such a possible result, by calling to mind the drain following its application to induration of the womb.

The application was continued, and in one year, very much to my surprise, the child was cured, the head being only a little, if any, larger than other children's of its age. Sutures were united. General health much improved. This occured in 1869, and in 1874 the child, with fair intellect and good health, was attending school. The parents leaving town, I have not heard from the child since. I was so much impressed with the result of this case, that I suggested the use of glycerine to Dr. Merrel of Monroeville, Ohio, who reported to our local Medical Association the result of a partial trial, as follows:

Case 2.—Child less than a year old; circumference of head, 22 inches; eyes much protruded, as well as the integuments over the separated sutures. Glycerine applied to the head, which was followed by a profuse flow of serum, so great, as to wet the pillow cases and most of the sheet, and in three weeks the eyes were restored to their natural position, and there was no protrusion between the sutures, but the head was not reduced in size by measurement. Treatment was to be continued. Dr. Merrel left Monroeville about this time, and I could learn nothing further of the case.

Case 3.—Friends reported this case to me, and I advised glycerine without seeing it. Its age was less than one year; had many convulsions; head very large. Glycerine tried as in the other cases, except that I recommended wetting cotton in glycerine, holding it in place by a tight-fitting cap. Discharge, same as in the other cases. No more convulsions, but the child died in a few weeks. In this case the head became sore while using the glycerine. The weather was very hot and the glycerine may have been impure. As this is one of the many incurable troubles, I thought I might be justified in reporting the trial of glycerine in these few cases, with the hope that a further trial in your hands may result in good.

Respectfully submitted,

Norwalk, Ohio.   A. N. READ.

REPORT FROM THE

SPECIAL COMMITTEE ON GYNÆCOLOGY

TO THE

OHIO STATE MEDICAL SOCIETY,

JUNE, 1876,

BY

THAD. A. REAMY, M. D.,

CINCINNATI.

Professor of Obstetrics and Clinical Midwifery and of Diseases of Children in the Medical College of Ohio; Gynæcologist
to the Good Samaritan Hospital.

REPORT FROM THE
SPECIAL COMMITTEE ON GYNÆCOLOGY

TO THE

OHIO STATE MEDICAL SOCIETY,

BY

THAD. A. REAMY, M. D.

REMOVAL OF THE NECK OF THE UTERUS FOR CANCER, WITH CASES.

In this paper I use the term *Cancer* in its general significance, accepting the view that usually the so-called varieties appearing in the uterus, at least, may properly be regarded as different stages of the same process. Whether the opinion of that eminent authority, Waldeyer, that all cancers are developed from epithelia, that when found in tissues anatomically devoid of epithelium, the origin has been from blastodermic remnants abnormally distributed, be true or false, the epithelial origin of cancer of the *uterus* will not be questioned. The opinion of Lawrence, that cancer is "cell necrosis," seems also quite probable. There can be no doubt that the discharge is largely from dead cells. The wonderful relief from pain which follows removal of the diseased mass, as verified in the following cases, also finds plausible explanation in the view of Lawrence that the pain of cancer is due solely to "reparative vital reactions, generally abortive, tending to throw off the dead parts."

Case 1.—In February, 1873, I was consulted by Mrs. B., aged 37, married, mother of four children, resident of Cincinnati. She was suffering severely of metrorrhagia. The menstrual periods were greatly prolonged, the quantity of flow exaggerated, and, as above implied, she had suffered within the last six months intermenstrual hemorrhages. The patient was only moderately anaemic. She complained of severe lumbar and pelvic pains, and a sense of "full-

ness " in the belly.   Recently she had had frequent attacks of
what had by her medical attendant been diagnosed uterine
colic.   She complained, also, of a burning sensation along
the course of the urethra.

A digital examination revealed the entire vaginal portion of
the uterine cervix to be indurated and nodulated, and characteristically hard.   This condition involved, also, to a slight
extent the anterior upper vaginal wall, though here not so
well marked.

The cervix was not immovable, though its mobility was
greatly limited, evidently from partial infiltration of the con-
nective tissue at the vault of the vagina.   At the left margin
of the os could clearly be detected, by the touch, a small ulcer,
whose edges presented the well known hard and brittle sensation.   The examination caused considerable loss of blood.
A visual examination, made four days subsequently by the
aid of Sim's Speculum, verified the " touch."

In order to further demonstrate the truth or falsity of my
opinions, a small portion of tissue was sliced off from the
margin of the ulcer, which was submitted for microscopic examination to my friend, Dr. H. A. Clark, a very competent
observer.   He found fibrous stroma, with ovoid alveolar
spaces, cells with large nuclei, compressed epithelial cells, etc.

Having determined the case to be one of epithelial cancer, the
removal of the cervix was advised.   Consent was granted.
Assisted by Prof. Clark and two of my students, I seized the
cervix with a strong vulsellum, dragging the uterus slowly
down as far as possible.   Owing, however, to the changed
condition of surrounding tissues, I was unable to bring the
os quite level with the vulva.   With a heavy, cutting gouge
forceps, one side of the cervix was now destroyed almost
to the cervico-vaginal junction.   The half stump then being
seized by the forceps, the other side of the cervix was removed to an equal extent.   Then, with a small-sized Simon's
scoop, the short remaining portion of the cervix was fun-
neled out completely to the os internum.

The mucous membrane around the upper portion of the vagina was now scraped off to a depth involving the submucous tissue, anteriorly removing the indurated nodules that were found pinning into the tissue. The parts being thoroughly cleansed, all the excavation was firmly packed with lint, soaked in a solution of bromine, one part to thirteen of alcohol. The vagina was then tamponed with cotton, soaked in a solution of bicarb. of soda. All the dressing was allowed to remain thirty hours. On removal, the parts were thoroughly washed out with a solution of chloride of sodium in warm water. The after dressing was lint, soaked in a solution of carbolic acid, one part to two hundred and seventy of proof spirits.

Results.—Complete recovery. The patient is now in the enjoyment of perfect health. Considerable cicatricial change exists in the upper portion of the vagina. The contractions in the anterior portion caused for a time some urethral irritation and inconvenience, but this has long since subsided. The cervix is, of course, quite short, but quite healthy, and the os is about normal in size.

Case 2.—Mrs. G., aged 41 years, native of Italy, resident of Cincinnati, consulted me in April, 1873. She was very anaemic; icteric coloring of the conjunctiva well marked. She was a widow, mother of two children, youngest 8 years old; husband dead four years.

She was now suffering of profuse hemorrhage per vaginam. She had been under treatment by several physicians during the past two years. Had suffered of uterine hemorrhage more than a year, which had grown much worse during the past three months. The discharge now was quite offensive. A digital examination per vaginam revealed the cervix more than half destroyed by ulceration. The uterus immobile, the vaginal walls, in almost all directions hard and nodulated. Indeed, all the upper half of the vagina was nearly filled with proliferated tissue. The caliber of the rectum was greatly encroached upon by the neoplasm.

Explaining to the patient and friends that the proposed operation was only for the relief of pain and the attendant distressing symptoms, and if possible to stay for a time the fatal march of the disease, but that finally death must be the result, consent was obtained.

With the gouge forceps, in a similar manner as in the preceding case, all that remained of the cervix to the os internum, also nearly all the tissue intervening between the vagina and rectum, including also most of the anterior vaginal wall, was removed. Then, with Simon's scoop, I carried the destruction in every direction, until there was left at several points but little more than the mucous membrane of the bladder and rectum. In scooping out the upper portion of the cervical canal, I should have mentioned that considerable uterine tissue was destroyed above the os internum. My aim was here, as it has been in all cases, to follow the cancerous growth wherever found, and this almost without regard to the extent of tissue involved—of course, limited by the boundaries of safety.

The growth in this case was medullary, greatly facilitating its removal.

After cleansing, the excavation was packed with lint, prepared as in Case I. The precaution was had, however, not to allow the packing to press directly against the walls, consisting only of mucous membrane. These were protected by lint. The after treatment was also the same as in Case I.

Results.—Hemorrhage at once ceased. Pain, which at the time of the operation, and for some time before, had been absolutely unbearable, was completely relieved. The cachexia, which was pronounced, rapidly disappeared.

This patient, who had emaciated to a skeleton, gained by the scales, within two months, fifteen pounds.

Further Results.—A recto-vaginal fistula of small size occurred just above the sphincter within three months after the operation, which, however, gave but little inconvenience.

The boundaries of the destroyed tissue in the main healed kindly. The patient enjoyed ten months of perfect health—absolutely free from pain.

Nevertheless, in fourteen months from the date of the operation, she died from the effects of the extension of the disease, involving the destruction of a large portion of the body of the uterus.

Case 3.—Mrs. S., residing near the Ohio River, a few miles above Cincinnati, was placed under my care in May, 1864. The patient was fifty years old, married, and the mother of six children, the youngest being 10 years old; no abortions nor miscarriages. She had suffered from menorrhagia for a year, which had within the past two months been almost constant and quite profuse. The discharge was also now offensive, and muddied in appearance by broken down tissue. She suffered frequent, sharp, unbearable pelvic pains. Digital and visual examination showed well defined cervical induration. From right and left lateral boundaries of the cervical lips, protruded nodular masses, characteristically hard. At two points, looking into the cervical canal, ragged-edged ulcers existed. Section of a nodule, extending back from the margin of an ulcer, was made, and the slice submitted to Prof. H. A. Clark for microscopic examination. He pronounced it cancerous. It presented, he said, in a marked degree, all the characteristic irregularly defined elements of structure.

Assisted by Prof. Clark and my pupils, Jackson and Mitchell, I removed the cervix in the manner above described, almost completely to the vaginal junction, scooping it out centrally to the os internum. After treatment, same as in other cases.

Results.—Perfect recovery. Has gained several pounds in weight; and was a few weeks since in the best of health.

Case 4.—Mrs. B., of Clinton County, Ohio; seen in consultation with her attending physicians, Drs. Morey and Lightner. The patient was nearly 50 years of age. The

ERRATUM.—CASE 3, in third line read 1874 instead of 1864.

disease had existed for a year when I saw her, which was in the spring of 1875. The cancerous growth had involved all the cervix, the recto-cervical and cervico-vesical portions of the vagina. Indeed, both rectum and bladder were severely encroached upon. The patient's suffering was intense. She suffered constant hemorrhage and was fearfully anaemic, unable to walk to any extent, even about her room.

The diseased mass was removed in the same manner as in other cases. Such was the extent, however, of the ravages made by the disease that I could leave in its removal scarcely more than the mucous membrane of the bladder in front, and that of the rectum behind; and though I followed the growth into the uterine cavity, I was of course unable to remove it all in this direction.

Results.—Perfect relief from pain and hemorrhage; arrest for a time of the progress of the disease; great improvement in general health, which continued six months and flattered the patient with ultimate recovery.

Ultimate Results.—Further progress of the disease, vesico-vaginal fistula; death. Drs. Mory and Lightner, very intelligent physicians of Clinton Co., had correctly diagnosed and prognosticated this case long before I saw it with them.

Case 5.—Mrs. R., of Portsmouth, Ohio, sent to me by my friends, Drs. Finch and McDowell, of that city. Patient married twice, 38 years of age. One child by husband of second marriage, about eighteen months old. Dated her illness from last labor. Involvement of about the same tissues and extent as in the last case. Microscopic examination was made in this instance by my colleague, Prof. Longworth, confirming the diagnosis, which was already painfully apparent. This patient was urgent for an operation. She was a beautiful and sprightly woman, and extremely anxious to live. When informed that the removal could not be complete, and could only be palliation, she added, " it might accomplish even more, and it must be done."

Assisted by Drs. Finch and McDowell, I removed the diseased tissues so far as possible in the same manner as in the other cases. I found the rectum thoroughly involved. Could leave nothing but its mucous membrane, and even then could not remove all the cancerous growth; neither was I able to reach it all in the direction of the uterus, as it had invaded that organ far beyond the os internum.

Results.—Relief from pain ; partial arrest of disease ; patient got about. Final results: a recto-vaginal fistula; progress of the disease, death six months after the operation.

Case 6.—Mrs. S., of Covington, Ky. Seen in consultation with my friend Dr. Henderson. Patient 44 years old ; a widow ; mother of several children ; youngest 16 or 18 years old ; had suffered uterine hemorrhage for the past six months. Irregular menstruation, vesical irritation and severe pelvic pain for more than a year.

Dr. H. had suspected cancer before I saw her. When we examined her together, already the crumbling-edged ulcerations had destroyed part of the cervix. The new growth filling up the cavity, and infiltrating the walls of the remaining cervical stump ; uterus immobile from infiltration at the vaginal vault.

The patient was sent by Dr. H. to the Good Samaritan Hospital in this city, and I removed the neck, assisted by my colleague, Prof. W. W. Dawson, much after the manner already detailed in the preceding cases. The dressing in this case was with a solution of carbolic acid instead of bromine.

Results.—Relief from pain; complete relief from hemorrhage; no special abatement of the disease. Operation was followed by septicemia, during the progress of which I had the rare opportunity of studying the natural history of septicemic fever. The patient being of homœpathic faith would take nothing prescribed. She got one dose, 20 grains, of quinia, perhaps on the 5th or 6th day after the operation, and was cheated with a smaller dose 4 or 5 days afterward. This constituted her internal medication for a period of several weeks. The temperature and pulse range was significant ; the temperature mounting to 107½° F. on several occasions, and reaching 106½° to 107° at some portion, not uniform, of each day for two or three weeks. The interesting and suggestive questions associated with this complication of septicemia I shall consider on another occasion, as these questions are foreign to the purposes of this paper. This patient finally lost the sight of one eye from choroiditis supervening upon the septic contamination.

The cancer progressed, involving the pelvic cellular tissue. She died of exhaustion, about six months after the operation, with probably not much relief from suffering nor prolongation of life as results of the operation.

Case 7.—Mrs. B., widow, aged 41 years ; mother of three children—youngest 16 years old—a resident of Cincinnati. Was seen by me, in consultation with her physician, Dr. Coulter, in February, 1876. She had been ill about a year. All the symptoms of cancer of the cervix had been prominently present for six months ; the pain, hemorrhage and dyscrasia well marked. So great was the suffering that the patient was using daily from six to ten grains of morphia. The vaginal portion of the cervix was almost completely destroyed ; the upper vaginal walls, and the pelvic cellular tissue adjacent, also involved. A mass of the growth protruded from the cavity of the cervical stump, which resembled very much uterine sarcoma.

I operated for the removal of so much as could be reached of the diseased tissue. Was assisted by Dr. Coulter and my son-in-law, Dr. Giles S. Mitchell. The mode of operation was the same as in the other cases. The involvement of the internal walls of the uterus about the os internum and above, to an unusual extent, and at some points—the disease being limited in this way mostly to the inner wall—was quite apparent. But at the upper portion of the vagina the disease vigorously extended out toward, and extensively involved, the cellular pelvic tissue.

These conditions were more clearly revealed as the operation proceeded. Diseased masses were in this case scooped
out at a point fairly above the os internum, at two points penetrating nearly to the serous wall of the uterus. Dressing,
same as in other cases.

Results.—Complete relief of pain ; cicatrization of all the
upper portion of the vagina, and at several points, indeed,
fairly around the margin of what, if there had been enough of
it left to entitle it to a name, would have been the cervical
stump. Extending half way over the thickness of the wall,
was developed what might easily have been regarded as
mucous membrane. In no case, amid such destruction, have
I witnessed such efforts at repair.

The patient so far improved as to be able to walk about
the house, and finally upon the streets.

Final Results.—Extension of the disease upward, involving
the body of the uterus, and penetrating its wall, the patient
finally dying,—probably of peritonitis,—months after the
operation.

REMARKS.—The foregoing cases are not recited for the
purpose of introducing new principles or discoveries, either in
the diagnosis, nature, pathology or treatment of uterine cancer. Indeed, as to the diagnosis and pathology, I have pur-
posely said barely enough to bring the cases clearly before
you. The rules adopted by this Society last year, restricting
within very brief limits all papers and reports offered to it,
under penalty of rejection by the Committee on Publication,
—to which rule, whether wisely or not, I stand committed—
have rendered these omissions necessary.

Again ; having no important discoveries to communicate in
this direction, is a still stronger reason why I should not
detain the Society. My object has been to furnish, briefly,
and almost without comment, some clinical work, that we
might together examine the testimony which it offers in con-
firmation or contradiction of principles already prominently
before the profession. Notwithstanding it is not yet well

11

settled whether cancer, attacking any tissue or gland, is curable by removal of the parts attacked, yet most surgeons recommend the practice. And certainly the removal of the uterine cervix under such circumstances—provided it can be done sufficiently early to include all the diseased manifesta-· tions, as is well known—is recommended by almost all respectable gynæcologists. The manner of removal, whether by galvano-cautery, écraseur, scissors, knife, or caustics, may be a matter of choice by the operator, or may justifiably be varied according to the peculiarities of individual cases. It is to the facility and safety with which the work can be done by the cutting gouge forceps, as practiced in the cases here reported, that I wish to call attention.

The instrument being narrow, the cutting edge at the distal extremities, it can be thrust into the diseased tissue in any direction, even including the uterine cavity, without danger to other structures. The instrument not being too sharp, the process of destruction partakes sufficiently of the nature of pincing to guard against hemorrhage, and to leave the parts in the most favorable condition for the action of the caustic when indicated, and for immediate granulation where' the caustic is not demanded.

I would by no means condemn galvano-cautery,—a method which includes, in one manipulation, destruction of diseased tissue and cauterization by heat of suspicioned tissues beyond. It certainly cannot be questioned that the application of white heat to the surface left, at the same moment and by the same means which removes the diseased mass, has in many instances been proven, clinically, to have advantages not inferior to those which so forcibly impress one, theoretically. But that these advantages are so great as to render the removal of the uterine neck by this means so much safer than by any other means, as to warrant the statement made by that very distinguished author and judicious clinician, Prof. T. Gaylord Thomas, to-wit: "He who performs the operation by other methods than by the galvano-cautery, should reflect that he is unquestionably lessening his patient's chances of life," I confess myself unwilling to admit. Moreover, the caustic by heat, to the extent of its practical application by this means, will, in but few cases, dispense with secondary cauterization by chemical agents. Since these must, therefore, usually be employed, I see no special advantage in the galvano-cautery.

I need hardly say to the members of this Society, that these opinions are founded upon careful observations made in a pretty large clinical experience.

If these views are correct, then, certainly, the simplicity of the method which I recommend is a matter of no small consideration; especially, when we consider the fact that, even with the best apparatus, the operator is often disappointed in securing the necessary amount of heat. And it adds no little to his embarrassment when the failure comes in the midst of an operation, and at a time when the necessary facilities for remedying the failure are not available. Again, it is not always easy to transport a battery of sufficient power in cases where patients have to be operated on at their homes.

Another object I have had, in presenting these cases is, to add their testimony to the immense advantage which follows the removal of cancerous tissue, even in cases so far advanced as to render recovery impossible,—advantages in the relief of pain, the arrest of the progress of the disease, and thus the prolongation of life. Thomas,* Munde,† Schroeder,‡ and others have highly commended the practice on these grounds.

Again. I wish to add the testimony of the first and third cases to the probability of the truth of the proposition that cancer is primarily a local disease, and therefore curable in at least a proportion of such cases as are seen early, when complete removal of all the morbid growth can be accomplished.¶

---

*Diseases Women, 4th ed., page 568. †Amer. Journal Obstet., August, 1872. ‡Ziemssen Cyclopœdia Med., Vol. x., page 291.

¶My friend and colleague, Prof. W. W. Dawson, informs me that he has had some very hopeful results from removal of the uterine neck, after a manner similar. In one case, at least, complete cure.

DISCUSSION ON DR. REAMY'S PAPER.

The paper of Dr. Reamy being the order for discussion, Dr. Ridenour, of Toledo, said :

This paper I regard as a very valuable and instructive one, in that it details a new mode of operation and treatment for a dreadful malady, in which all plans of treatment hitherto tried have failed to cure or arrest. In two of the cases reported by Dr. Reamy, so long a time has elapsed since the operation, without a return of any symptom of the disease, as to allow the Doctor to indulge a hope that in these cases a radical cure may have been effected; while' in the other cases, such an alleviation of pain and other disagreeable symptoms, and improvement in the general condition of the patients, was accomplished as to fully justify the operations made, and render the report an extremely interesting one.

I have had no personal experience in the treatment of this class of cases. The preparation of brómine used is new to me, as also the manner of removing the diseased structures by the cutting gouge forceps and scraping.

Speaking of instruments, I would like to ask the surgeons and gynæcologists who are here, what is their present opinion of the écraseur as a useful and convenient instrument in the operations to which it is adapted ?

I was surprised to hear Dr. Atlee, at the recent meeting of the American Medical Association in Philadelphia, denounce it as a barbarous, inconvenient, and dangerous instrument, which should be discarded entirely, and for which the knife and other cutting instruments, or the galvanic cautery should be substituted.

My use of the instrument in question has been almost entirely confined to the removal of fibrous tumors and polypi from the uterine cavity, and has been satisfactory. In the first case in which I used it, which was also my first operation for the removal of fibroids, the tumor was attached to the interior surface of the fundus ; depended perpendicularly ;

was extremely dense and hard, almost cartilaginous in consistence; was four inches in length by one and one-half inches in diameter, with a short neck one inch through, attached to the center of the fundus. It was removed with the wire écraseur; the stem passed up to the top of the womb, and the wire, encircling the tumor, bent at a right angle with the stem.

In this operation I had an illustration of the liability, mentioned by Dr. Dunlap, of the cutting of the wire by the sharp edges of the stem, since this accident occurred, rendering it necessary to remove the instrument and replace the wire by a new one.

In this case, I knew of no other means by which the tumor could have been safely removed. The uterine cavity was completely filled, the tumor projecting about half an inch beyond the external os.

I have had no experience with the wire rope.

Dr. William Mussey, of Cincinnati, said:

I have employed the galvano-cautery pretty extensively, and in many cases I regard its use as invaluable. I am by no means, however, confined to its use in such cases. As to one of the cases reported by Dr. Reamy, if I am not mistaken as to the recognition of the case from his description, and the locality of the patient, I saw her not long before her death, although I am not sure that Dr. Reamy had knowledge of my seeing her. It was my opinion that she was dying of peritonitis, possibly induced by the action of the bromine-caustic penetrating the peritoneal cavity.

Dr. Reamy replied:

I was not aware that Dr. Mussey had seen this patient, but am certain, from the gentleman's high professional integrity, and the jealousy with which he protects the code, that if he saw her (and I am now certain he did), it was in a legitimate way. The patient had peritonitis at the time of death, but that it was induced by bromine is quite a mistake. It is well known that the development of peritonitis from progress of the disease is quite a common occurrence, and such was the fact in this case. The application of bromine in caustic strength had not been made for months before death.

Dr. J. W. Hamilton, of Columbus, said:

I have been deeply interested in this paper and its discussion; the more deeply interested because my friend Dr. Reamy has been more fortunate in results than myself. Some years ago I removed the neck in a few cases, but the results were not such as to warrant me in a repetition of the practice. I am in the habit now of employing simply palliatives in these cases, as the end in unmistakable cases is pretty uniformly death.

Dr. Scott, of Cleveland, said:

I have been much interested in Dr. Reamy's report. I must say, however, I have been somewhat surprised at the fearlessness with which he destroys tissue. I can understand how his mode of removing the cervix may be admirable, and that this can be done with comparative safety, but when the proposition is made to remove tissues back to the rectum, forward to the bladder, and upward, even involving part of the uterus itself, I cannot understand how it can be done with safety. I will not say it cannot be done by the gentleman, whom I know to be a dextrous operator, but I should myself shrink from it. I see these cases, have had some experience in their management, but I never attempt removal. I confine my practice to the use of caustics in suitable cases; but my usual plan is palliation. I restrain the hemorrhage, correct so far as possible the offensiveness of the discharge, and, above all, so far as can be done, relieve the pain. But as I have not considered these cases curable by any means, I treat them in that view, and so inform the friends of the patient.

I think we are hardly justified in making further efforts in an incurable disease. As before remarked, however, the report of Dr. R. is full of suggestions, and the results he has obtained challenge our careful study.

Dr. Reamy being called upon by the President to close the discussion, said :

Mr. President : I have but little to add to the brief report which the society has done me the honor to hear and my friends to discuss. Some explanatory comments, however, may be in order.

As stated in my report, my object is to give simply some clinical experience. Of course, the cases here given do not include a large proportion of the cases which have come under my care during the past twenty-three years. Indeed, they do not include all the cases of this frightful disease which have come under my charge in hospital and private practice during the period covering the cases. They simply embrace the cases treated in the manner specified, and are given solely for the purpose of illustrating the results of the treatment. Should I live till next year, I hope to finish the report, by other cases which have had other plans of treatment at my hands. When this is completed we shall have the opportunity of studying the results of treatment more closely, so far as my own individual experience goes. These cases already number thirteen not included in this report.

The doctrine that cancer is a local disease, and therefore curable by removal, as is well known to all, is very old. And although long since abandoned in most respectable quarters, still, I think all will agree with me that at the present moment the doctrine is rapidly gaining ground, and certainly bids fair soon to be thoroughly established in the minds of many leading pathologists. I mean the doctrine of local origin, which does not, of course, necessarily carry with it the curability by removal, or complete destruction of cancer cells. Still, the first being proven, the latter looks so probable that, as suggested by Dr. Robert Barnes, of London, it is "a most hopeful doctrine; one to which the clinical physician should cling as that which most encourages therapeutical research, and which alone holds out a prospect of ultimate triumph over the disease." Not only does modern research point to the extreme probability of cancer being of local origin, but to my own mind, studying the subject from a clinical point, the impression is equally strong that in a large proportion of cases the first steps toward the disease have their origin in traumata. In this view we probably have some clue to the marked preponderance of married over single women who suffer of cancer of the uterus. And possibly in this and the modes of dress, may be found some reasons for the frequency of cancer of the breast in women. These views are familiar, and are frequently referred to by writers.

On the question of traumatic cause, I have a few suggestive facts, which I have obtained from patients suffering from uterine cancer; incidents of personal history, which we have not time, nor is this the proper place to relate, but which are instructive and may be given in another way.

I am not prepared to pronounce fully for the local origin of cancer, but I confess myself as strongly impressed with its truth. I think that here, as in the study of many other diseases, the pathologist must be to a large extent aided by the clinician in the final settlement of the question.

Though such observations may be censurable, considered empiricism in the estimation of some, to me there is no such objection. In the present state of medical science, much of our most available knowledge is empirical.

As all know, and as admitted in this paper, amputation of the neck of the uterus for cancer is quite old. From the time it was first suggested by Larivariot in 1780, and performed by Osiander in 1801, to the present, it has been practiced. And at the present time it is recommended by most respectable writers, especially when it can be done early.

chroeder, whom I have already quoted, in his recent work on

Diseases of the Female Sexual Organs, warmly commends it. And he commends it even in cases too far gone for any hope of cure, for the relief of pain and arrest of the disease.

To my mind the marked improvement that follows removal of the diseased mass thoroughly, either by caustics or otherwise, the arrest for a time of the disease, and often concomitant with these, the marvelous improvement in constructive metamorphosis of tissue, marked by a rapid gain of strength and weight, have a significance as to the nature of the disease,which has not yet been fully appreciated by clinicians and writers, and which challenges our closest analysis.   I am aware that marked improvement occasionally occurs, apparently without any special treatment whatever, and even that spontaneous cures are reported in a few instances on apparently good authority, but such cases are painfully rare, and they, in no way, materially, affect the above statements.

Unfortunately, in the vast majority of cases, especially where the uterus is the seat of cancer, the lymphatic glands which are so abundant in this locality, and which are probably largely concerned in the production of the systemic dyscrasia, are already hopelessly involved, long before the unfortunate patient is examined by the medical man. · If it should prove finally, clearly true that the disease is local in origin, and curable, of course the importance of early operations will be more prominent than now.   And I think we may console ourselves, that as an offset to what those of us who are specially interested in the clinical gynæcological field, must have observed as a growing evil in some quarters, viz : a speculum examination of almost every woman who complains, we may find some compensation in the earlier detection of these cancer cases.   At any rate we should carefully watch for them.

The heroic practice which I have followed in carrying my removal of the diseased mass in all directions, even into the body of the uterus and to the mucous membrane of the bladder and rectum, in some cases, calls upon me pretty thor-

ough criticisms from my much esteemed friend, Dr. Scott.
I have only to say, this constitutes an important feature of
my practice.

Regarding the putrid mass, the cancer cells, as the con-
centration of the enemy, I attack it wherever found ; so far as
possible, follow it with the destroyer wherever it has gone.
Tissue which has been attacked by the disease is no longer
of any practical use, and may as well be at once removed.
Even in the earlier changes, the tissue is only thè harbor for
the nests of cells which are ever ready to invade and
destroy. Of course, care must always be had not to open
the peritoneal cavity ; in the posterior spaces especially must
care be exercised ; nor to open into the bladder, nor destroy
the urethra. These directions must be approached with
caution. But there is not so much danger as a study of
these parts in a healthy subject would indicate. Follow the
disease vigorously and fearlessly. By the method I adopt, I
have had no special trouble in any case from bleeding,—a
danger which might deter those who have not operated.

Schrœder recommends removal in these cases as extensive
as my own. It is gratifying to have endorsement from such
high authority. It is but proper to remark, however, that
all my cases but one had been treated before his contribution
to Ziemssen's Cyclopœdia appeared. Of course it will be
understood that I am now referring to removal of the diseased mass in cases where no cure can be looked for in consequence of the advanced stage.

The use of bromine as a caustic, in these cases, was, I
believe, first made by Dr. Routh, of England. It is now
pretty generally employed, and has with many won the envia-
ble reputation of destroying cancer cells. Schrœder is in the
habit of injecting it into tissues infected by cancer cells,
and securing their removal by sloughing. In the same manner precisely, he injects it as is recommended by Broadbent to
use acetic acid.

It may have been noticed, the solution I use is by no means
so strong as that recommended by Schrœder and others.

Schrœder uses one part of bromine to five of alcohol; I, one part to thirteen of alcohol. By allowing the lint to remain longer in contact with the surface, I have found this strength to be quite sufficient to cause disintegration of cancer cells, and not so dangerous to other tissues. Another reason why I may use a weaker solution is, that I remove the cancerous growth more thoroughly with instruments than most operators, therefore leaving much less work for the caustic to do.

I am not prepared to say that no other caustic will answer as well as bromine. Many others are in general use. I can only say that from this I think I have seen more satisfactory results.

Finally, I cannot agree with the plan which has been advocated in this discussion to-night by two of my friends, viz: Abandon these cases as incurable, attempting only to relieve pain and render the patient in this way as comfortable as possible. In doing this, we fail to bring to our patient one of the strongest elements of comfort, namely, hope; even hope of recovery. It is my deliberate conviction, that in this disease, even in a case where the fatal end must, to the mind of the medical man, be an inevitable reality, it is his bounden duty to work with a vigor and confidence that in its very nature inspires hope in the doomed sufferer. No disease is more depressing in its effects upon the victim; no disease is more cruel in the pain and suffering which it forces upon its subjects. Often it lasts for many months, and even years. To inform the patient, therefore, early in an attack that she has cancer, and that it is incurable, is needlessly and cruelly to add to her torture, and in many cases to shorten her days. I would not, of course, withhold from trusted friends, the husband, for example, the nature of the disease. I would leave it to his judgment at what period before the final issue to communicate the sad and terrible news.

The condition of the mind, the moral surroundings, have much influence upon the rapidity with which this disease destroys life. Everything, therefore, that can be properly done to improve these conditions, should be considered as a part of the general treatment. Pain should be relieved, of course, by the direct use of anodynes when necessary. The highest office of the physician is not always filled when he has simply medicated his patient. Nor of the surgeon when he has used the knife. Part of his work is moral, spiritual. Moved by a true sympathy for the sufferer, a sympathy which is deepened and strengthened by intelligence and culture, the true physician comes into the sick chamber, perhaps already darkened by the shadow of approaching death, as a ray of light, as an angel of hope. His words are those of kindness and good cheer.

The unfortunate victim of cancer often needs the exercise of these qualities in her physician to a degree scarcely reached by the subject of other maladies. Doomed to suffer, and dying by progressive disintegration, her descent to the grave should be rendered as smooth as possible. Never should she be made to feel that she is abandoned to the cruel destroyer either by physician or friends. And then the physician should work constantly under the stimulus of the knowledge that even desperate cases may possibly recover. He should always keep in mind the light of the truth that the time will yet come when cancer, timely treated, will prove generally curable.

Plate 1 represents the instruments employed in the operations referred to in the text.

1. Sims' Speculum.

2. Vulsellum.

3. Gouge Forceps, straight.

4. Gouge Forceps, curved.

5. Simon's Scoop.

PLATE I.

1

2

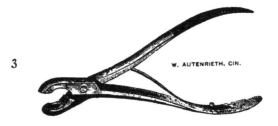

3

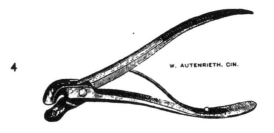

4

5

FOREIGN BODIES IN THE RECTUM,

—BY—

C. S. MUSCROFT, M. D.,

Surgeon to the Cincinnati Hospital and to St. Mary's Hospital.

FOREIGN BODIES IN THE RECTUM.

BY

C. S. MUSCROFT, M. D.

Surgeon to the Cincinnati Hospital and to St. Mary's Hospital.

But few writers on surgical treatises have omitted to mention foreign bodies in the rectum, some relating many interesting cases, others, but few, while almost no mention is made of the subject by otherwise eminent writers, and this may be said of authors who have written excellent monographs on the diseases of the rectum.

As a rule, it is very rare to meet with foreign bodies in the rectum, and most of my surgical friends with whom I have conversed, have never met with a single instance in their own practice. Among the surgeons of this city I have not learned of more than three.

It is astonishing what a very great variety of foreign bodies have found their way into the rectum, either by accident or design; sometimes by the unaccountable wish and act of the patient, sometimes by the vicious and malignant design of others. The largest collection of cases of this kind is reported by Paul F. Eve, M. D., professor of surgery in the medical department of the University of Nashville, Tenn.

Many more cases not related in this paper, can be found in surgical works and the different medical journals, but enough are given to illustrate the great interest and importance the subject is entitled to.

Foreign bodies find their way into the rectum by three different modes. First, they may lodge there after being swallowed and passed through the other portions of the intestinal canal, and may consist of pieces of bone, pins, needles, nails, sealing-wax, cinnamon bark, rings, ferrules, cherry stones, peach stones, plum stones, pieces of gristle, tendon, coins, of ivory, metal, or cork, and many other substances. Secondly, they may form in the intestines themselves, by diseased action from some kind of food, such as oat-meal, or of medicines, as magnesia, and constitute what are called intestinal concretions. Sir Benj. Brodee mentions a case of concretion of magnesia in the bowels of a lady patient that weighed three pounds. Parr in his medical dictionary, mentions a case in which a calculus having formed in the intestines, was found in the rectum. These concretions sometimes consist of gall stones in large quantities, &c. Third, they may be introduced through the anus for the purpose of relieving constipation, or may be forced in by malicious intent, while the person is sleeping from the effects of inebriation, or they may be introduced for the purpose of committing suicide, and may consist of bottles, pots, cups, a knitting sheath, a shuttle with a ball of yarn, a pig's tail, tumblers, a beet, a forked stick, a teacup, a diamond breast-pin, a piece of reed, &c.

Ashton says, "Foreign bodies that have been swallowed, do not usually occasion much inconvenience in their passage through the intestinal canal, though it is sometimes marked by considerable irritation. Should the substance not be discharged with the fæces, but become entangled in the rectum, it will give rise to inflammation, accompanied by tenesmus, violent straining, (bloody stools), and perhaps prolapsus, by perforation of the tissues of the intestine it will lead to the formation of abscess and fistula, or partial or total obstruction may be produced, followed by enteritis or peritonitis. These effects will be greatly influenced by the size, form, shape, and nature of the substance. When intestinal or fæcal concretions are the cause, the symptoms are gradual in their accession, and are preceded by signs of derangement of the stomach, liver and bowels ; at first, the local disturbance is marked by a feeling of weight, distention, and pain in the rectum, followed by obstinate constipation, great straining to relieve the bowels, attended with more or less prolapsus of the mucous membrane, and congestion of its vessels, and if the patient be not relieved, enteritis, peritonitis and death will ensue. When the foreign substance has been introduced through the anus, the symptoms are more rapid in their development, and the bowel has at the same time been injured, they will be more or less serious in their character in proportion to the extent and nature of the lesion.

In the fourth edition of the system of surgery, by Prof. S. D. Gross, he says, the *extraction* of foreign substances from the rectum, the surgeon is governed by the circumstances of each individual case. In general, when they are not situated too high up, they may readily be removed by the finger, or with a pair of forceps, the anus being previously dilated with the finger or speculum. Large alvine concretions may require to be crushed before they can be withdrawn, but such an expedient can rarely be proper, much less the division of the sphincter muscles. Should the latter, however, become necessary, on account of the extraordinary bulk of the foreign body, its awkward shape or slippery surface, the incision should be made in the direction of coccyx, as less likely to cause hemorrhage and other mischief. When the substance has slipped very high up into the bowel, the extraction may be aided by counterpressure upon the hypogastrium, thereby steadying the extraneous body, and enabling the surgeon to take better hold upon it. To render the pressure effective, the bladder must previously be emptied. Sharp, rough, pointed, or spiculated bodies may require to be sheathed before removal, to prevent mischief to the mucous lining. In the celebrated case of Marchetti, a strong cord was secured to the projecting extremity of the pig's tail, after which a

12

piece of reed was slipped over it into the bowel, which was thus defended from injury. An anal speculum, or hollow bougie, open above, would answer a better purpose, or, in absence of this, a large rectum-bougie might be used. A long bone, stretched obliquely across the bowel, with the ends firmly imbedded in its walls, may require to be broken at its middle before it can be removed; or, if it is very thin and not too hard, it may be cut in two with a pair of scissors, and each piece extracted separately.

Hardened fæcal matter should be softened by repeated injections of warm water, or some mucilagenous fluid, and afterwards extracted with a scoop, or spoon, or handle of a long slender pair of lithotomy-forceps. The operation may also be performed with a very stout, double wire, bent into a hook at the extremity, or what is frequently better than' all, the fingers. Ascarides may be dislodged in the same manner, or they may be destroyed by filling the rectum with some stimulating liquid, as a mixture of spirits of turpentine, aloes, or garlic juice, a popular remedy, often employed with much benefit.

Dr. Geo. Bushe, of New York, who is the highest authority upon the early literature of diseases of the rectum, says: "The instruments necessary for extracting these bodies, are blunt hooks of different sizes and shapes, a lever, gimlet, cutting forceps, strong scissors with probe points, a six-inch narrow saw, wooden gergeret, polypus and lithotomy forceps of different shapes and sizes, a speculum, strong waxed ligatures, metallic tubes of various length and size, and probe-pointed bistoury," to all of which, the crooked finger and small hand are admirable adjuncts.

The doctor narrates the following case. Having placed the hips of a delicate lady over the edge of the bed, and bent her knees toward her chin, while she lay on her back, he introduced a strong and long lithotomy forceps, with which cautiously laying hold of the concretion, he slowly and steadily extracted it, with no more injury than slight laceration of the mucous membrane, although on measurement it proved to be- (a large concretion) six inches and three quarters in circumference, and two inches and a half in length.   The bowels were then freely evacuated by injections, leeches and fermentations were applied to the anus, the recumbent position was enjoined, and a speedy recovery ensued.

In his valuable monograph, he relates the following cases: Saucerotte withdrew a piece of wood, three inches in length and two in width, with a cork-screw, which he inserted into the wood, while he steadied it with the forefinger of his left hand.   Bruchman performed a similar operation with a gimlet.   Bushe.

Nolet, surgeon to the king of France, and Marine Hospital at Brest, relates the following curious case : A monk wishing to get rid of a violent colic, introduced into the rectum a bottle of Hungary water, (these bottles are generally very long,) through the cork of which, he had made a small opening to permit the fluid to flow into the intestine.   In his anxiety to perform the operation well, he pushed the bottle so far that it completely entered into the gut.   He could neither go to stool or receive a lavement.   A *sage femme* failed to insert her hand ; the forceps and speculum were tried in vain ; however, a boy, from eight to nine years of age, succeeded in introducing his hand, and removed the bottle.   Idem.

Dessault, in endeavoring to extract a porcelain jelly-pot of a conical form, and about three inches in length, which had been introduced for eight days, placed on two opposite points of its diameter two strong pincers, which however fractured it so that he was compelled to extract the pieces in succession.   He might have been less fortunate had the substance been glass.   Idem.

Morand reports the two following cases : A man about sixty, presented himself at the Hospital de la Charité, complaining that the pipe of a syringe had entered his rectum, and he could not discharge it. Gerard introduced his finger and felt the foreign body, which he removed with a lithotomy forceps. It proved to be a large knitting sheath of box-wood about a half a foot long.

A weaver about sixty years old, who for a long time had suffered from constipation, having heard vaguely of the efficacy of suppositories in children, introduced a shuttle furnished with its roll of yarn into the rectum. After five days, being unable to withdraw it, he presented himself at the Hotel Dieu for assistance, when Bonhomme extracted it with a lithotomy forceps, aided by his finger. By injections, fomentations and leeches, the cure was completed in twenty days. Idem.

Hevin relates the two following cases: M. Quesnay pushed a bone, which was arrested in the œsophagus, into the stomach. Afterwards this body presented itself near the orifice of the rectum. The patient, tormented with pain, called on Quesnay, who introduced his finger into the anus, and found the bone placed obliquely across the gut, with its inferior extremity fixed into its walls. He passed a forceps along his finger, and having seized the bone superiorly, lifted it up, thus disengaging its inferior portion. He then grasped it lower down, and removed it without difficulty or pain. Idem.

Faget was called to see a man who complained of severe pain in the fundament and bladder, with retention of urine. On examination of the rectum, he found a foreign body situated transverseley, and fixed firmly into the intestine. He introduced a forceps, seized and easily withdrew this body, which proved to be a mutton bone, about as thick as a quill, seventeen lines long, and sharp at both extremities. The patient had swallowed it eight days before. Idem.

"Méeckren mentions a case, in which the jaw-bone of a Turbot, of great length, was arrested in the rectum."

After giving the symptoms, which were much the same as in the above case, "he extracted it with his fingers, the process being both difficult and painful. The patient remembered that he had swallowed it eight days previously." Idem.

Thiandière details the case of a man aged twenty-two, who, with a view to overcome costiveness, introduced a forked stick into the rectum. This stick was five inches long, one prong was an inch and a half longer than the other, and they were separated to the extent of two inches, each prong being about four lines in diameter, and the stem formed by their union about half an inch. He inserted the stem first, and when the short prong had entered the bowel, he endeavored by dragging on the long one to force out the indurated fæces. In this ingenious essay it is unnecessary to say he failed completely. The pain being very severe he ceased the manipulations, and, finding it impossible to withdraw the fork; he forced the long prong completely within the anus, with the extraordinary idea that it would be consumed with the food. Fearful to divulge the nature of the case, he bore his sufferings in solitude and dispair until the abdominal pain and difficulty in urinating led him to seek the aid of Thiandiére, who, on making an examination, soon discovered the foreign body, but it was so high up that he could scarcely touch it. He endeavored, but in vain, to extract it with a forceps passed through a speculum. The happy idea then struck him of introducing his hand, which, having washed out the rectum, he insinulated finger by finger. Conducted by the long branch, he succeeded in reaching the bifurcated stick, and disengaged it with difficulty from a fold of the mucous membrane, in which it had become entangled, then compressing the prongs together, he safely removed it. Idem.

Méeckren also mentions a case which occurred to Tho-luix, in which the jaw bone of a fish was situated across the rectum. This surgeon cut it across with a scissors, and then extracted the two portions with ease. Idem.

In the Miscellanea curiosa sive ephemer, adad, natur, curios, dec. III, ann. II, obs. VIII, we read of a case in which a similar course was pursued for the extraction of the jaw bone of a dog. Idem.

Moreau mentions the case of a woman aged thirty-four years, who, for a long time, but particularly for four years, had labored under a sensation of considerable weight in the fundament. Her complexion was pale and at times yellow; she was subject to frequent attacks of colic, and her stomach was so weak that it scarcely retained any nourishment. Her efforts to defecate were sometimes so considerable that they were followed by convulsions and cold perspiration. So much did she dread the efforts, that she resisted the calls of nature, and consequently seldom had a motion oftener than once in fifteen days or three weeks, when she moderated the violence of the bearing down pains, and facilitated the issue of the fæces, by resting the fundament on a round stick. On examining the rectum, he perceived a solid body, apparently of large volume. He injected almond oil into the intestine, and then introduced a lithotomy forceps, with which he seized the concretion; but in the extraction it broke; however, the fragments were easily removed. This concretion was of the size of a large pippin. Idem.

Zacutus Lusitanus records a case in which a leech, about to be applied to a hæmorrhoid, made its way into the rectum. He injected onion juice into the intestine, and the leech was soon discharged, almost dead. He recommends injection of ox gall or castor in similar cases. Idem.

Richard Quain, in his valuable monographs of the diseases of the rectum, mentions the following cases:

Morand says, a gentleman who had suffered habitually from constipation, "by the advice of a practitioner whom he consulted in Paris, daily introduced into the bowel a piece of flexible cane (about a finger's thickness), where it was allowed to remain till the desire to evacuate fæces came on." For more than a twelve month this plan succeeded; but at length, having been passed hurriedly, the stick "was sucked into the body," and it slipped beyond reach. It was in seven days; after that the surgeon was called. The lower end of the stick was beyond reach, but it was touched with a bougie, and the opposite end was "felt projecting midway between the illium and the umbilicus on the right side," and here the slighest pressure caused pain. The stick was removed by means of the hand passed into the bowel.

A man aged 32 had suffered for a considerable time from nausea and vomiting. In the middle of the abdomen was a tumor, lumpy on the surface and movable under the pressure of the hand. He died with peritonitis. The lower end of the illium, which was dilated into a pouch as large as the head of a fœtus, contained 120 kernels of plums and cherries, and 92 bullets. Idem.

A female aged 41, well formed, of good intelligence, mother of several children, had been attacked at intervals with sickness and vomiting, sometimes blood. In examination of the body, pins were discovered in the stomach, weighing nine ounces; and in the duodenum, where they were lightly packed, the quantity found amounted to about a pound in weight. The pins were bent head and point together in a thimble, from which they were taken with the tongue. It was ascertained that the person had a habit in her childhood of eating starch and slate pencils. Idem.

Mr. Quain says, in 1842 the late Mr. Bolton Hodgson, of Chesham, a clear-headed and skillful practitioner, sent him a preparation taken from the body of a person, in whom death had resulted from the opening made by a pin in a large artery. Then follows the history of the case, and the artery wounded was found to be the commen illiac.

As an instance where a foreign body in the rectum may cause stricture, Dr. Barlow recorded the following: A female aged 46, was admitted into Guy's Hospital, having suffered from constipation during thirteen days. Here follows the symptoms of the case, but I will only mention the *post mortem* appearance of the rectum. Recent lymph was found, gluing the intestines together ; a stricture was discovered at the commencement of the rectum, ten inches from the anus ; it had a greenish color and it was very hard ; it admitted the passage of the little finger, and contained a small fish bone. The intestine above the stricture was distended with fluid ; the remaining viscera were healthy. Idem.

Another fatal case of stricture of the rectum, four inches from the anus is also mentioned, which was caused by a small fish bone an inch in length, apparently that of a flounder.

Still another fatal case of stricture, the result of a small fish bone, at the distance of six inches from the anus, is mentioned by the same author, and is preparation 1255 in the Museum of the College of Surgeons.

The last case he mentions says, a gentleman applied to the second Monro "on account of a large flat tumor in the cellular substance of the sphincter, which created much uneasiness." He was not relieved, but in "eighteen years afterwards the patient perceived a small hard substance, which proved to be a small bone."

In Velpeau's Operative Surgery, edited by the late Prof. Geo. C. Blackman, gives some interesting modes of procedure for removing foreign bodies from the rectum.

He says: *Calculi*, giving rise to constipation, have been extracted from the rectum by Schmucker, by means of the forceps; and also by the ordinary forceps after having broken them up, by Chambon and M. Miller. J. S. Buzzoni removed from it a coffee cup by means of a whale bone busk.

Plater says seriously, that a mole, introduced alive into the rectum of a peasant, had become so strongly attached to it that it could not be extracted, except by drawing upon its tail after having killed it. Idem.

M. Cazenave was obliged, in one case, to extract a broken gourd from the rectum. Idem.

A pestle which could not be withdrawn without difficulty by means of the forceps, caused rectitis and death in a patient of M. Dor, who succeeded better in another case in extracting a fork, the teeth of which were directed downwards, and who states that he removed a cologne-water bottle in a third patient by means of Hunters forceps. Idem.

Wm. Ferguson in his treatise on practical surgery, says that Mr. Russell, of Aberdeen, relates a case in the Medical Gazette for the 19th of August, 1842, of an individual who seemingly has a remarkable propensity for introducing stones within the anus, he (the patient) himself had extracted, after the surgeons had failed, one weighing thirty two ounces, and another had been removed with midwifery forceps by Dr. Moir six months previously, weighing twenty-nine ounces. In the same journal, February, 1842, there is a case related, where Mr. B. Phillips extracted, after the patient's death, a portion of a walking stick, and several examples of a similar nature are referred to.

Although it does not belong strictly to the subject of foreign bodies in the rectum, I will relate the following cases, reported by T. J. Ashton, of injury to the part. He says by awkward attempts and the application of too much force in endeavoring to pass a bougie up the rectum, its tunics have been torn or perforated. By ignorant and clumsy nurses, enema pipes have been thrust through the rectum and peritoneum, and the fluid injected into the abdominal cavity. In the museum of St. Bartholomew's Hospital is the preparation from the body of a patient whose death was occasioned by the perforation of the rectum by a metallic clysterpipe and the injection of a pint of gruel into the peritoneal cavity. In the same museum are two other preparations of the rectum, uterus, and vagina, and the large intestines of a child. Ten months before her death, in an endeavor to administer an enema, a clysterpipe was forced through the adjacent walls of the rectum and vagina. At the part thus injured, there is a small depression in the wall of the vagina, and a long, pale, and irregular cicatrix in that of the rectum. Near the cicatrix, also, there are traces of small healed ulcers of the mucous membrane of the rectum. Just below the cicatrix, at the distance of about an inch from the margin of the anus, the canal of the rectum is reduced to an eighth of an inch in diameter, and the adjacent tunics are indurated. Above this stricture the intestine is greatly dilated, and contained a large bucketful of fluid fæcal matter.

Ashton says, Bushe mentions having seen a case of perforation of the recto-vaginal septum by the end of an umbrella on which the patient was in the act of sitting. He also says the rectum is sometimes perforated by unskillful attempts to introduce a catheter into the bladder, and relates a case where "he discovered the point of the instrument had been thrust through the urethra immediately anterior to the prostate, and has passed into the rectum."

Ashton says "the position of the patient (submitting to the removal of a foreign body from the rectum), should be on the side, with the knees drawn up towards the chin and the buttocks projecting over the edge of the bed or couch, or, if deemed more convenient, he may be placed in the same position as for the operation of lithotomy."

He removed an ivory tube from the rectum of a woman, which had been forced into it while receiving an injection; he saw the patient within half an hour from the time of the accident; on making an examination, the tube was felt immediately above the margin of the internal sphincter, it was extracted without difficulty, a pair of œsphagus forceps being used for the purpose.

In another patient, a physician, he removed a piece of bone having very sharp angular corners, and says, if it had not been removed early, doubtless it would have perforated the intestine.

He says, in May, 1853, Mr. Lacy of Pool, removed piece-meal from the rectum of a lady, a concretion, "at least fifteen inches in circumference." The outer part of it consisted of concentric layers of what looked like red sandstone, and which proved, on examination, to be a compound of iron and magnesia. The interior was a softer mixture of the earthy ferruginous matters with many thousands of strawberry and other seeds.

Mr. Jones, of Llandyssul, removed three concretions from the rectum of a farmer, two of them were as large as a man's fist. "The concretions consisted of layers of a substance of a brownish color, much harder than leather, each of them containing a plum-stone for a nucleus."

Tuffell, in 1813, removed a flask of crystal from the rectum, but was obliged to break it, before he could accomplish the removal. Idem.

Constance mentions the case of a man who fell on an inverted blacking-pot, and the whole of it forced up the rectum. Attempts were made for an hour and a half to dilate the sphincter, and remove it with a forceps, but in vain. The small end of an iron pestle was then introduced, till it touched the bottom, and being held firmly was struck with a flat iron. At the second blow the pot was broken into several pieces, which were removed piece by piece, by the forceps or fingers. Next morning he labored under severe intestinal inflammation, with incessant vomiting and excruciating pain all over the whole belly ; he died at night. The pot was two inches and three eights in diameter at the brim, an inch and a half at the base, and two inches and an eighth in depth. Idem.

Another case is quoted where a Greenwhich pensioner introduced a large plug of wood into the rectum for the purpose of stopping a diarrhoea, where it remained eight days. It was with great difficulty extracted by Mr. Mc-Laughlan, surgeon to the Greenwhich Hospital. Idem.

In June, 1842, a man aged sixty, was brought to King's College Hospital, laboring under obstruction of the bowels, which he attributed to having eaten a large quantity of peas six days previously. He expired while being carried in a chair up to the ward. On examining the body after death, upwards of a pint of gray peas was found in the rectum. They had been swallowed without mastication, and had undergone no alteration in passing through the alimentary canal, except becoming swollen by warmth and moisture. The urethra was pressed upon, and he had retention of urine for four days. The bladder was enormously distended, its apex reaching the umbilicus, and its base nearly fitting the brim of the pelvis. Idem.

Mr. Lawrence had a case in which a man had broken the neck of a wine bottle into his rectum; he gradually dilated the sphincter, introduced his whole hand, and removed it. Idem.

Mr. Ferguson removed a bougie from the rectum of an old gentleman who was in the habit of using such an instrument; on one occasion he passed the bougie within the sphincter, and could not withdraw it. Several unsuccessful attempts had been made to remove it, previous to Mr. Ferguson seeing the patient; with some difficulty he succeeded in seizing the end with a pair of lithotomy forceps, and withdrawing it. The bougie was nine inches in length and an inch in diameter. Idem.

The following case is taken from Practices and Principles of Surgery, by H. H. Smith, M. D., of Philadelphia: In a case reported by Ruschenberger, of the U. S. Navy, where a glass goblet, three and a half inches high, with a brim two and five-eighths, and a base one and seven-eighths inches, was introduced into the rectum of a chinaman. The whole was removed by Parker, of Canton, by crushing it with a strong forceps, protecting the parts with folds of cloth, and removing the smaller fragments with a teaspoon, and a similar treatment would be requisite for the removal of all fragile articles. The particulars of the above case are given in the collection of remarkable cases in surgery, by Paul F. Eve, M. D., Nashville, Tenn., from which also the following cases are taken. In most of the cases related in the Dr.'s book, the particulars of each case are given at considerable length, but as this paper is intended merely to give the case, the minutiæ are omitted, unless great interest be added by the process and circumstances of their removal, and the instruments used.

The following being a case of more than usual interest in all its features, is transcribed in full:

A tin tumbler pushed by the patient into the rectum; then passed into the colon; failure to remove it, and death of the patient.

The patient introduced the tumbler on the 4th of April, 1834, causing its entrance into the bowel by sitting upon it. The tumbler being drawn upwards with the returning intestine, attemps were made by the patient to extract it, with his fingers, and by means of a "shoemaker's forceps." With these he had considerably broken and flattened the edge of the base or rim of the tumbler, and forced it beyond the rectum into the colon. It was found in this position by the physician, who summoned Dr. George Moode, of North Andover, Mass. Dr. M. introduced his hand and forearm into the rectum, seized the tumbler, and made a powerful, but unsuccessful effort to extract it. The blunt hook was next tried, without extracting the tumbler, although it was brought down so that it could be seen. Owing to its flattened state, it hitched in the plicæ of the intestine. Several physicians and surgeons were called in consultation; among others, Dr. Joseph Kittredge, of An-

dover, and Dr. Whiting, of Haverhill.   No efforts at extraction by the hook or fingers were of any avail; although
the tumbler was brought into view and seized, powerful
efforts being made to disengage it from its situation.   One
of the practitioners again introduced his hand, but could
not bring the tumbler away.   The patient asked to have
his abdomen opened, and the foreign body thus removed.
He was told that this would produce certain death.   A
proposition to divide the levatores ani was negatived by
Dr. Kittredge, who feared fatal hemorrhage.   The patient
lived about three days after this.   His tongue sloughed,
and there was gangrene of the large intestine.   The tumbler was extracted after death; it measured 3½ inches in
length, 3½ in width in the direction of the flattened part,
and 2 inches across its base, it would hold nearly three
gills.

An immense number of plum-stones (about two hundred and eighty) removed from the rectum, by R. Hazel-
hurst, M. D., of Brunswick, Georgia.

The patient was a strong negro, aged about 25, who
took into his head to eat very freely of plums, stones and
all, as he says, (and probably truly), without eating anything else during the day, and at two different times he
was ordered to take a dose of castor-oil, which not producing the desired effect, I had recourse to artificial means,
the introduction of the fore finger with the intention of
scooping them down with it.   The rectum was so sore that
he could not bear the slightest pressure.   Four or five were
removed by several injections of cold water, and six or
seven with the finger.   Another dose of oil was given the
next day which brought away some more, and purged him
excessively; he was seen on the third day when he was
suffering greatly.   The rectum was completely plugged up
with the stones, only allowing liquid fæces to pass through
their interstices.   Having run away, he was again found on
the fourth day, when found, he was lieing on the ground,

so much reduced from hunger and suffering, that he was unable to move, and had to be carried home. There was no time to be lost. I had him tied, introduced my finger, and sliding a pair of forceps, rounded and grooved at the extremities, alongside, was steadily employed, for the space of three hours, in removing the plum-stones one by one, until one hundred and thirty were counted, besides some forty that passed afterwards, and more before, which were not counted, but must have made them altogether amount to two hundred and forty. The extraction of each stone occasioned exquisite pain. Most of them were covered with blood. Dysenteric symptoms ensued, which ceased with the removal of the cause and appropriate treatment. By measurement it is found that he must have eaten almost ten quarts of plums, say a peck at a moderate calculation. Idem.

Dr. Horace Nelson, of Plattsburg, New York, removed a cow's horn, five inches long, from the rectum of a patient with a strong pair of forceps. Idem. ,

M. Maisonneuve relates the case of a man, a patient of M. Cloquet, who had introduced a tumbler into the rectum. In order to extract it, M. Cloquet dilated the anus with six fingers, which, being insufficient to dilate it to the required extent, M. M. Maisonneuve and Huguier, who were present, each added four fingers. The *fourteen fingers* enlarged the anal orifice to such a degree as to allow the tumbler to be seen; the bottom of the tumbler was directed upwards, the open part downward. The man was then told to bear down, as if in defecation, and the glass was expelled. This case is a remarkable example of the extent to which the anus may be dilated without injury to the sphincters. Idem.

M. Cloquet also removed a Flemish *beer glass* (shaped like our champagne glasses), from the rectum. The glass was seized with the forceps, but broke into many pieces.

In order to get the lower part out, it was found necessary to turn it, as the open broken part was turned downward. The man died in a few days. Idem.

Dupytren removed a square preserve pot from the rectum, the open part being superior. He seized hold of the rim by means of a blunt hook covered with chamois leather, and thus extracted it. Idem.

T. M. Harris, M. D., of Harrisville, Virginia, removed from the rectum of a patient a half pint flask, which had been introduced to relieve an attack of piles. The instrument used was a pair of forceps made somewhat after the fashion of the obstetrical instrument, with blades about seven inches long, by about three-fourths of an inch wide, and handles eight or ten inches long. This instrument he improvised and had made for the occasion. The instrument, however, slipped from the bottle, after being well greased and introduced, one blade at a time. He then broke the bottle and removed the glass piece-meal, requiring three hours to accomplish his object.

In about nine months afterwards he removed a beet seven inches long from the rectum of the same patient, by means of the forceps which he had had made for his first operation. Idem.

A large piece of wood was removed from the rectum after remaining three days. The manner of the operation is not mentioned. It was seven inches long and seven inches in circumference where two projecting knobs, each as large as half a fowl's egg, had formed the commencing division of two new branches. It was removed by a pair of obstetric forceps, which, when grasping it, the dilatation extended to ten inches in circumference as they passed out from the rectum. The stick had been introduced, with a view, by the process of rubbing, to disperse a stone in the bladder. Idem.

Another case is mentioned where no name is given, (both of these were copied from the Lancet, the first for

1835 and this for 1849), where an accumulation of fish bones in the rectum had caused death by hemorrhage. Idem.

This case is so important that it will not admit of the slightest abbreviation:

In December, 1848, a peasant was admitted into the hospital of Orvieto, in the last degree of feebleness and prostration. Under the idea that he would save the trouble and expense of eating, he had plugged his rectum with a piece of wood. This was nine days previously. Many attempts were made in the interval to relieve him of the awkward predicament, but without success. After his admission, M. Riali, of Italy, reiterated these attempts, but their only effect was to force the foreign body further from the outlet, and to increase the impaction; already this body had passed beyond the reach of the finger. In the circumstances it was determined to expose the descending colon by cutting through the abdominal parieties. Having done this, the attempts were made to force the piece of wood from the termination of the colon, at which it was distinctly felt into the rectum, and so downwards, and again without success. An incision was therefore made into the bowel, and the foreign body—the dimensions of which were about six and one-fourth inches, by one, and the form of a bluntish cone—was extracted through the opening. The edges of the wound in the intestine and parieties were united by suture and cold applications placed over the usual dressings. During the first few days there was much flatulent distention of the abdomen, with considerable sickness and vomiting, for which symptoms three bleedings, three applications of leeches, and some doses of croton oil, were thought necessary. The bowels acted on the fifth day; the wound had healed on the fourteenth, when the patient was well, though for the sake of prudence he was kept two months in the hospital. And now, two years and nine months afterwards, he continues well,

13

eating and drinking all before him, and no longer disposed to distress himself on the ground of his appetite.   Idem.

The following case is of so much notoriety, that it has been mentioned in nearly all the works on surgery, and particularly those of diseases of the rectum :

A party of debauchees, (students of the University of Göttingen), wishing to play a trick upon a woman of pleasure, cut short the bristles of a pig's tail, which they forcibly introduced into her rectum, the thick end upwards. Severe pain was the immediate consequence ; the mucous membrane was irritated or perforated by the bristle stumps, and tenesmus set in ; a portion of three inches in length projected beyond the anus.   The patient's state was very distressing.   M. Marchettis was called upon on the sixth day.   He conceived the idea of preparing a piece of cane so as to introduce one end of it into the rectum, and thus isolate the foreign body from the wall of the intestine. He then attached a firm cord to the end of the pig's tail, which was passed into the tube; the latter was gently pushed up into the rectum, and when its extremity had reached beyond the extremity of the foreign body, both were extracted together without difficulty or pain.   The patient felt immediate relief, and all unpleasant symptoms, the vomiting and fever, quickly disappeared.   Idem.

Another case, which happened to Prof. Van Reinlein : the point of a bit of wood could be felt under the false ribs, and the respiration was extremely difficult and painful.   The portion of wood was extracted with a forceps. Several inflammatory symptoms followed, but they were removed by proper treatment.   Idem.

Dahlencamp removed a piece of wood that had been driven into the rectum by accident, after remaining a year and producing fistulous abscess.   Idem.

In one case Desault was forced to break up a chimney sweeper's scraper with a lithotomy forceps and then extract it.   Idem.

Kern and Walther have each extracted a shoemakers' pincers from the rectum.   Idem.

Tumor in the rectum containing the debris of a fœtus ; exterpation :

M. Bouchacourt, chief surgeon of the Charité of Lyons, communicated to the Academy of Sciences, on the 26th of August, 1849, the case of a little girl, six years of age, from whom a tumor of the rectum was exterpated, which contained the debris of a fœtus.   This case belongs to the *endocymian monsters* of Geoffroy St. Hilaire.   Since the case related by Velpeau, in 1840, this is the only monstrosity of the kind which has required a surgical operation. The tumor was removed by excision and ligature.   Idem.

The following letter addressed to me explains itself:

CINCINNATI, May 29th, 1876.

My Dear Doctor :—I offer the following contribution to your collection of cases of foreign bodies in the rectum. Only interesting as showing the cunning device of a patient suffering from delirium tremens.   Some years ago I was attending a well-known and popular merchant in this city for an attack of delirium tremens.   At my early visit one morning, I asked him how he felt; he replied, I would feel very well if it was not for all those pins in my fundament.   I asked him what he meant; he said, my *back-side* is full of pins and they annoy me greatly.   Thinking some local irritation had given direction to his hallucination, and that a pretended effort to remove the pins would remove the foolish impression, I directed him to turn upon his side, and I would take them all away; upon separating the buttocks and closely examining the anus, I discovered, to my utter astonishment, just visible, what appeared to be the point of an ordinary pin—seizing it with a pair of forceps, I succeeded after a good deal of resistance from the sphincter, and pain to the patient, in extracting a *large cluster diamond breast-pin,* which I recognized as one that usually adorned his bosom. Holding the pin before his eyes, I asked him how it happened to have been in so strange a locality. After a moments bewildered gaze, his countenance brightened up, and he told me that during the night his room was full of robbers, taking everything they could lay their hands on, and seeing his jewel sparkling in his shirt-bosom, he hastily removed it, and placed it in what he considered a safe hiding place. The patient recovered from his delirium tremens, and experienced no inconvenience from the presence or removal of the foreign body, and to the day of his death, which occurred some years subsequently, the jewel glittered on his bosom, an amusing reminder to those of his acquaintances who knew its strange history.

Truly your friend,

A. S. DANDRIDGE.

Some years ago an old German woman, aged about 70, was placed under my care for treatment at St. Mary's Hospital. She had suffered for many months from the effects of procedentia uteri. When I saw her, a large part of the uterus extended beyond the vulva. . Previous to the prolapse of the uterus, she was subject to constipation of the bowels, attended with tenesmus. This condition she thought had produced the state of the uterus already mentioned, and to relieve it, (after trying many different medicines), she had been persuaded by some of her friends, to introduce into the rectum a tube made of reed, or common fishing-pole, about ten inches long, and three quarters of an inch in diameter. At least one-half of the tube was in the rectum and was retained by tapes fastened to bandages round the body and hips. When presented to me, she had worn this tube for about three weeks, the parts being in a very filthy and disgusting condition, and at the same time appearing ludicrous in the highest degree. I told her before I could do anything for the womb, it would be necessary to remove the pipe from the.rectum and cleanse the parts, so that I could make a proper and thorough examination. This however, she positively refused to do, saying if the tube was taken out, her bowels would become stopped altogether and she would never be able to get them open again, and rather than submit to an examination and treatment, left the hospital.

In the class of injuries above narrated, on account of the many serious complications and difficulties attending the removal of foreign bodies from the rectum, as well as their various forms, there are no cases in surgery that more urgently call into requisition the mental resources, sound judgment, inventive ability, prompt action and dexterity of the operator.

A CASE OF

"TUMEUR AERIENNE,

(SO-CALLED);

FOLLOWING THE REDUCTION OF A

Sub-Glenoid Dislocation of the Head of the Humerus,

—BY—

W. H. MUSSEY, M. D.

A CASE OF "TUMEUR AERIENNE,"

(SO-CALLED);

FOLLOWING THE REDUCTION OF A SUB-GLENOID DISLOCATION OF THE HEAD OF THE HUMERUS

—BY—

W. H. MUSSEY, M. D.

———

Linn Boyd, aged 21 years, on August 30, 1873, fell from a stairway—from the top to the bottom—and struck the elbow of his left arm against the brick wall upon which the steps were constructed; the head of the humerus was thrown downward, under the glenoid cavity. On standing up, the hand reached below the knee-joint.

Dr. Haile was called and came immediately to the case, finding a dislocation of the head of the humerus. He placed the patient upon the floor, placed a towel around the arm —which was controlled by two men, who made the required extension—and placing his heel in the axilla, proceeded to manipulate. The head of the bone was found to slip easily into the glenoid cavity. When the heel of the operator was removed there was an immediate enlargement of the shoulder apparatus, commencing in the axilla, and forward under the pectoral muscle, extending under and above the clavicle in the neck and under the scapula. Under these circumstances I was sent for, and found, half an hour after the occurrence, an enormous tumefaction of the whole region, with loss of pulse at the wrist, numbness in the hand, and great pain in the shoulder. These symptoms indicated a rupture of a vessel of some kind, and a very large extravasation of blood.

The expectation was, that I would cut down and tie the subclavian artery. Having previously expressed my con victions that such a procedure, in such cases, was illadvised and hasty, and even unnecessary in a large majority of cases, I determined to watch the case and treat it without ligature, for a time at least. The patient was removed to his home in Newport, Ky.; evaporating lotions were applied, cardiac sedatives were administered, the bowels kept freely open, and the case carefully observed. The pulsation of the radial artery was fully established the next day; the skin of the shoulder was very tense, but there was no untoward symptom. The third day the skin relaxed a little, but there was considerable constitutional disturbance. After a gradual subsidence of the swelling from day to day, and no untoward symptoms presenting for ten days, I was easy as to any question of the propriety of the course I had adopted, and in three months the use of the arm was restored—the use of electricity having been resorted to, to relieve the infiltration of the tissues, the stiffness of the muscles, and the numbness of the nerves. The arm has never been so strong as before the accident, and is a little smaller than that of the opposite side.

I mentioned this case to Surgeon Norris, of the U.S. Army, who detailed a case, occurring at the Soldiers' Home in Washington City, where a similar accident occurred, in the person of an old soldier, following repeated and protracted attempts at reduction. When the infiltration took place, the patient was so feeble that it was deemed unwise to ligate the subclavian artery. This prostrated condition lasted for days, and the symptoms were not alarming or requiring interference, so no operation was performed and the patient gradually regained strength, but not the use of his arm. Pulsation in the radial artery became apparent, though it was very feeble, in about one year from the injury.

In the *Western Lancet*, September, 1856, page 469, the late Prof. Blackman communicated the details of a case in which he tied the subclavian artery, which was fatal on the separation of the ligature. He voluntarily said to me the day after ligation was performed, that he did not believe that the subclavian artery had been ruptured, but that some other vessel had been injured. He acknowledged his haste in his conclusion to operate.

In the *Medico-Chirurgical Transactions*, vol. XXIX, page 23, 1846, the late John C. Warren, of Boston, details an interesting case of a like character.

Dr. Blackman, in his paper, has grouped a large number of similar cases well worthy of perusal.

HOT SPRINGS,

ARKANSAS,

—BY—

PROF. E. B. STEVENS, M. D.

University of Syracuse, N. Y.

HOT SPRINGS, ARKANSAS.

BY PROF. E. B. STEVENS, M. D.

University of Syracuse, N. Y.

The whole of Garland county, Arkansas, is made up of a series of spurs of the Ozark Mountains. Here and there we find contracted intervales, with good soil ; but for the most part the country is barren and exceedingly wild and broken. But still, some of the most picturesque landscapes in the world are to be seen in almost every direction. It will naturally occur to the visitor here, to wonder how these things were ever discovered,—hid away, as they are, amongst the mountains, and even until quite recently of such difficult access —it must have been the most chance accident that revealed their locality and developed their properties. But, briefly, the geography and general surroundings of what has come to be known as the "*Hot Springs*" of Arkansas, are almost indescribable.

The main street of the city occupies a narrow valley, which has Hot Springs Mountain on the east and a similar mountain on the west. These two mountains run almost parallel, north and south, for nearly a mile. Traversing this valley there is Hot Springs Creek—a rapid stream that serves as an open sewer for the valley with its hotels, stores, shops saloons, bath-houses, &c.

From the west side of the Hot Springs Mountain, gush out the thermal springs, perhaps about fifty in number, and they have a temperature of from 93° to 150°. This hot water is utilized by being conducted in iron pipes to the various bath-houses which are conveniently located along the margin of the creek at the base of the mountain.

Climate.—The climate here is delightful ; nowhere in this country can it be surpassed, either for the invalid or the well person.   There is, to be sure, a long warm season, with ver little winter.   But not only is this long stretch of warmth desirable for the invalid, but it is wonderfully relieved, both for the sick and well, by the refreshing nights.   It is very rare that blankets will not be required before morning.

Cases.—Almost every form of chronic ailment comes here for treatment.   But especially chronic rheumatism, syphilis, cutaneous diseases (both simple and specific), neuralgia, and various nervous affections, make up the great bulk of those who seek relief at the Hot Springs.   And I am now prepared to report, that a *very large per cent.* of these patients go away either absolutely cured or greatly improved ; and this result is to be coupled with the other fact that, *almost all* of these patients only come here after persistent and long time treatment at home by the ordinary legitimate modes.

Mode of using the Water.—The bath- houses ,are fitted up so that : 1st. You can have a general bath in the tub, the temperature being under control by hot and cold faucets, and this temperature is directed by the physician just as he writes a prescription to the druggist—both as to degree of heat and time to stay in.   When the patient comes out he is wiped and rubbed and shampooed very vigorously by the bather. Or, 2nd, there is an apartment for a hot.vapor bath.   The patient usually enters this after a brief stay in the tub.   The temperature of the vapor is about 105° to 110°, and the patient remains in the vapor 3 to 5 minutes.   Or, 3rd, after he vapor, sometimes the patient is put in "*pack*," to encourage very profuse sweating. This consists of putting the patient back in the tub and wrapping him well with blankets.

Medical Treatment Here.—Many patients who come here *confine* themselves to the internal and external use of the hot water, either with or without professional advice ; but by far the large majority enter upon regular medical treatment in connection with the baths. And it is simply wonderful the immunity with which people will use mercury, arsenic, potash, &c., in this way. The water evidently acts as an eliminative to such an extent that the usual irritant and destructive effects of these agents are not experienced.

Results.—It would be singular, indeed, if, with the extreme character of the cases which come here, many persons should not go away—disappointed. Of course, some come here as a *dernier*, who can be regarded only as incurables. Some come here under mistaken notions of their own condition and the adaptability of Hot Springs to their cases. [Most persons should consult their own physician, and either direct, or, better, through their physician, consult some reliable man here, before undertaking the expense and fatigue of a journey to this place.] But, as already said, despite these drawbacks, I have been greatly surprised at the large per centage of cures effected here

"Ral City."—One of the very interesting features of Hot Springs is what is known here as "Ral City." A large population is constantly here of poor, miserable paupers, suffering with all manner of ailments. In their poverty they occupy cheap board shanties that cover the face of Hot Springs Mountain. These citizens of the "Ral" take their ablutions at the "Ral Hole," or the "Mud Hole," bathing-pools enclosed near the origin of the Hot Springs, and drink direct from the Springs. They depend on charity—offals of hotels, "soup houses," &c.,—for food; they rarely have any medical advice or medicines; and yet a large number of these poor people are restored to health. I have myself taken the trouble to watch quite a number of them, and have been surprised to see such favorable results—under so adverse circumstances. These results are, in my opinion, very strong evidences,—perhaps the strongest,—of the therapeutic value of these waters.

14

Rationale of Curative Effects.—I am not prepared to say what, if any, peculiar medicinal properties these waters have; their analysis does not suggest anything specially important.* And yet there would seem, from the results, to be some alterant influence afforded; with most persons their is diuresis; and Dr. Lawrence claims that the laboratory of this mountain imparts a certain degree of magnetism to the hot water. It is quite certain that the hot water, as it first gushes from the springs, is quite different from the same water cooled and subsequently re-heated. But aside from these considerations, the use of pure water of various temperatures —cold, tepid and hot,—or of medicated waters, is as old as medicine,—as old as revelation. Undoubtedly the use of this hot water, either with or without medicine, has been thoroughly systematized at this place. The patient, of course, has the advantage of cleanliness, and the skin is soon placed in its most healthy condition; processes of sweating, together with the rubbing, kneading and shampooing, encourage processes of absorption and elimination; the skin, the kidneys, probably all the secreting organs, are brought into lively action.

Then, too, the strict attention, which most physicians here enforce, as to diet; the restraint from various dissipations, late hours, and fashionable excesses, all contribute largely to favorable results. So, too, the entire change of habits, change of climate, freedom from care, and novelty of scenery, all these doubtless have their share in the results which are observed.

The Amount of this Hot Water, which a person may comfortably drink is wonderful; with most persons hot or tepid water, produces nausea and vomiting if taken into the stomach freely. This thermal water produces no such effect, a person may absolutely fill his stomach to repletion without discomfort, indeed, it speedily commences to pass away again by the kidneys.

The Alcohol and Tobacco Appetite.—There is no question but that the poor unfortunate victim of appetite, either of whisky or tobacco, or both, *can*, *if he really desires*, overcome these appetites easier here than any place in the world.

The free use of the baths, and drinking the water, not only tends to a rapid elimination of these poisons which have accumulated in the system, but at the same time actually *suspends* the *desire for their use*, so that the familiar phrase at this place, of "boiling the whiskey out of a man" is literally accomplished. I have seen this verified so positively that I deem it very important to present to the profession.

Indeed I have seen patients under treatment for various chronic diseases, who have assured me that immediately after commencing the use of the waters, that one of the incidental results was to *completely suspend all desire for alcohol.*

As very many intelligent physicians are skeptical as to the value of the Hot Springs, I have been somewhat guarded both in making my observations thus far, as well as in the foregoing record. I only in conclusion fortify my views with a quotation, bearing upon the subject, from that very excellent authority, Mr. Fuller, in his well known work on Rheumatism. [See page 332, Philadelphia, Ed. 1864.]

" Under these circumstances, says Mr. Fuller, recourse must be had to the various thermal springs, with which nature has endowed both this country and the continent, as if for the relief of the disease in question, (rheumatism). When everything else fails, they not unfrequently afford extraordinary and permanent relief. Whatever the modus operandi of the waters, their free use both internally and externally, exercises a beneficial influence, which is in vain sought from medicine and bathing in other places. The effect produced is at once sedative and tonic. The pain-worn sufferer, irritable and anxious, repairs to the springs unable to sleep, and troubled with dyspepsia, connected with a sluggish condition of the skin, liver, kidneys and bowels. After ten days, or a fortnight's trial of their virtues, he begins to find himself less irritable, less anxious, and less wakeful ; he sleeps more soundly, and feels more refreshed by his sleep, his digestion improves, the whole system is invigorated, and after a time, the excretory organs act so much more efficiently that it becomes unnecessary to have recourse to medicines for their relief. Coincidently with this increased freedom, in the various channels by which the excretions are carried out of the system, and with the greater purity of blood, which consequently ensues, there is observed a decrease in the articular symptoms, which arise, as I have shown, from a vitiated condition of the circulating fluid. There is no fresh accession of pain or inflammation, no recurrence of synvoial effusion, no increase of thickening about the joints. On the contrary, the enlargement gradually subsides, and by the assistance of the water, applied in the form of douche, whereby local friction is combined with fomentation, the stiffness disappears, and the patient to a great degree regains his former activity.

" It might be supposed that the importation of the various waters, would render a visit to their source unnecessary. But such is not the case. The natural waters may be taken regularly at home, and diligent use may be made of baths containing the same constituents in solution, but the effect is far different from that observed during a residence at the springs. The vast importance of the total change of scene, and air, and habits, consequent on a visit to the English or Continental watering places, can hardly be over estimated ; a new stimulus is imparted to the system, the organic functions receive an impulse which cannot be communicated to them in any other way ; *and remedies which have proven unavailing at home, very shortly become active agents for good.* Indeed, it is a question, whether the benefit derived from a visit to any of the thermal springs is not attributable almost as much to this sort of influence, as to the medicinal action of the waters."

LIST OF

DECEASED MEMBERS

OF THE

OHIO STATE MEDICAL SOCIETY,

With Date of Admission and Date of Death.

NAME.	P. O. ADDRESS.	ADMITTED.	DIED.
Ackley, H. A. . . .	Cleveland . .	1850	
Allen, Peter, . . .	Kinsman . .	1850	
Amos, C. E. . . .	Cleveland . .	1852	
Andrews, F. M. .	Dayton . .	1862	*Army.*
Angel, E.	Akron . . .	1852	
Arnold, Emil, . .	Ironton . .	1873	
Baker, A. H. . . .	Cincinnati . .	1846	1865
Baker, Timothy H.	Wooster . .	1851	1871
Ballard, H. D. . .	Findlay . . .		1871
Blackman, G. C. .	Cincinnati . .	1860	1871
Boyle, C. E. . . .	Columbus . .	1851	1870
Boalse, A. N. . .	Lockburn . .	1848	
Boerstler, G. W. . .	Lancaster . .	1846	1871
Brown, B. S. . .	Bellefontaine .	1855	1873
Brown, E. T. . . .	Logan . . .	1849	
Bronson, James, .	Newton Falls	1852	
Brennan, Thomas, .	Dayton . . .	1855	1858
Bridge, W. W. . .	Marion . . .	1859	1864
Baggs, James, . . .	Ontario . . .	1866	1868
Buckner, Phillip J. .	Cincinnati . .	1850	
Buckner, Wm. . .	Hamilton . .	1853	
Butterfield, John, .	Columbus . .	1846	1847
Carey, Abel, . . .	Salem . . .	1852	1872
Carroll, Thomas, .	Cincinnati . .	1854	1871
Caldwell, Joseph, .	Huron . . .	1857	1866
Chamberlain, E. K.	Cincinnati . .	1847	1847
Conner, P. S. . . .	Cincinnati . .	1853	1854
Cook, Charles C. .	Youngstown .	1862	1863

NAME.	P. O. ADDRESS.	ADMITTED.	DIED.
Cook, F.	Atwater . . .	1853	1857
Cox, D. A. . . .	New Paris . .	1846	
Crook, James M. . .	Dayton . . .	1853	
Crume, P. M. . .	Eaton . . .	1847	1869
Dawson, John, . .	Columbus . .	1851	1866
Danna, M. . . .	. . . . .	1849	
Dean, W. F. . . .	Milan	1857	*Army*.
Dean, G. A. . .	McComb . .	1874	1875
Delemater, John, . .	Cleveland . .	1850	1867
Dodge, I. S. . . .	Cincinnati . .	1854	1872
Doherty, G. A. . .	Cincinnati . .	1868	1873
Dolman, Wm. . .	Cleveland . .	1852	
Ells, G. E.	Lithopolis . .	1849	1867
Foote, H. E. . .	Cincinnati . .	1854	1871
Fries, George, .. .	Cincinnati . .	1862	1866
Fyffe, E. P. . . .	Urbana . ..	1851	1867
Gabriel, R. W. . .	Dublin . . .	1854	1860
Gailey, J. D. . .	Marion . . .	1851	
Gans S.	Cincinnati . .	1861	1864
Gard, B. F. . . .	Columbus . .	1847	1849
Gatson, E.	Morristown . .	1849	1868
Gille, L. C. C. . .	Westville . .	1853	
Green, M.	Cambridge . .	1855	1856
Griswold, Wayne, . .	Circleville . .	1866	
Haggott, J. P. . .	Eaton . . .	1861	1862
Haines, Job, . . .	Dayton . .	1853	1860
Haines, V.	Cambridge . .	1853	1865
Hall, W. C. . . .	Fayetteville .	1859	1872
Helmick, G. W. . .	Harrisburg . .	1848	
Henderson, W. . .	Delaware . .	1848	1866
Hopkins, Rudd C. .	Newburg . .	1852	*Army*.
Hornbeck, L. . .	New Carlisle .	1849	1865
Howard, R. L. . .	Columbus . .	1846	
Hughes, J. W. . .	Berlin Center	1858	1869
Hurxthall, F. T. . .	Massillon . .	1849	
Johnson, Wm. . .	Delaware . .	1850	
Judkins, J. P. . . .	Cincinnati . .	1846	1867
Judkins, Wm. . .	Cincinnati . .	1847	1861
Kable, W. R. . . .	Bellebrook . .	1846	1859
Kennedy, J. L. . .	Batavia . .	1864	1866

NAME.	P. O. ADDRESS.	ADMITTED.	DIED.
Kineman, J. W. . .	Ashland . . .	1870	1874
Kreider, M. Z. . .	Lancaster . .	1846	1852
Kyle, J. G.	Xenia . . .	1856	1870
Lathrop, H. . . .	Columbus . .	1846	1849
Lawson, L. M. . .	Cincinnati . .	1853	1864
Marshall, N. T. . .	Cincinnati. .	1854	
Martin, Joshua, . .	Xenia . . .	1853	1857
Matson, A. F. . .	Logansville .	1857	1867
McCracken, W. A. .	Springfield . .	1867	
McGuire, W. B. .	Waynesville .	1848	
McMeans, R. R. . .	Sandusky . .	1854	1862
McNeal, F. D. . .	Canal Dover .	1854	
Metz, Abram, . . .	Massillon . .	1852	1875
Mendenhall, G. . .	Cincinnati. .	1854	1874
Merriman, A. . . .	Madison . . .	1853	1867
Mitchell, G. F. . .	Mansfield . .	1850	1869
Mitchell, M. . . .	Mansfield . .	1863	1864
Millikin, Samuel, .	Hamilton . .	1853	
Moore, Jonas, . . .	Marietta . . .	1852	1856
Morehead, W. . .	Zanesville . .	1855	1861
Mount, William, . .	Cumminsville .	1853	1866
Mussey, R. D. . .	Cincinnati. .	1847	1866
Naw, J. H. . . .	Carroll . . .	1873	1875
Norton, J. C. . .	Marion . . .	1848	
Oliver, J. Q. . . .	Cincinnati . .	1854	
Pease, L. T. . . .	Williamsburg.	1863	1874
Potter, J. F. . . .	Cincinnati . .	1854	1868
Purple, J. G. . .	Brooklyn . .	1853	
Putnam, J.	Gahn. . . .	1873	1873
Reid, J. T. . . .	Fairfield . .	1864	1864
Risinger, J. F. . .	Galion . . .	1849	1866
Rigdon, L. . . .	Hamilton . .	1853	1865
Rives, L. C. . . .	Cincinnati . .	1850	1870
Rodman, Thomas S.	Cleveland . .	1852	
Robertson, James, .	Perrysburg . .	1853	1854
Russell, I. W. . .	Mount Vernon	1848	1876
Sachse, G. J. . . .	Columbus . .	1846	1860
Sanders, Moses, . .	Norwalk . .	1853	
Shotwell, John T. .	Cincinnati . .	1850	1850
Shædford, R. J. . .	Midway . .	1853	1868

NAME.	P. O. ADDRESS.	ADMITTED.	DIED.
Sheppard, W. A. . . .	New Vienna .	1856	1872
Silver D. H.	Columbus . .	1851	1864
Skinner, J. S. . . .	Columbus . .	1849	
Sharpe, E. C. . . .	Williamsburg .	1859	1868
Smith, Edmund, . . .	. . . . . .	1850	1850
Smith, A. C. ✓ . .	Medina . .	1852	1861
Smith, J. A.	Piqua . . .	1853	1858
Smith, S. M. . . .	Columbus . .	1846	1874
Spillman, Henry, . .	Medina . . .	1855	1862
Stanton, Benjamin, .	Salem . . .	1852	1861
Story, R. . . . . ✓	Cleveland . .	1852	1866
Taggart, T. M. . .	Dalton . . .	1857	1867
Taliaferro, Wm. T. .	Cincinnati . .	1854	1871
Tappan, Benjamin, .	Steubenville .	1852	
Thompson, M. . .	Mount Vernon	1850	1867
Thompson, Robert,	Columbus . .	1846	1865
Thompson, J. W. .	Columbus . .	1860	1862
Thomas, K. G. . .	Alliance . .	1858	1869
Tilden, D. J. . . .	Toledo . . .	1850	
Tilden, Daniel, . .	Sandusky . .	1856	1870
Tullis, J. W. . . .	Troy	1851	
Van Pearse, James,	Columbus . .	1850	
Van Tuyl, D. R. . .	South Bend . .	1850	
Van Tuyl, H. . . .	Dayton . .	1853	
Wallace, R.	Lewisburg . .	1861	1865
White, John, . . .	. . . . . .	1848	
Wigton, A. E. . . .	Delaware . .	1861	1862
Weatherby, ʻA. S. .	Cardington .	1865	1870
Woody, Robert. . .	Eaton . . .	1863	1872

LIST OF
MEMBERS
OF THE
Ohio State Medical Society,
WITH P. O. ADDRESS AND DATE OF ADMISSION.

NAME.	P. O. ADDRESS.	ADMITTED.
Adams, D. P.	Columbus	1873
Adams, John M.	Lebanon	1874
Adams, John W.	Lebanon	
Adams, John M.	Ridgeville	1874
Agard, Aurelius H.	Sandusky	1858
Aiken, P. J.	Newark	1869
Alcorn, A. W.	Ravenna	1870
Allen, Dudley,	Oberlin	1870
Allen, D. B.	West Liberty	1865
Amick, M. L.	Cincinnati	1874
Anderson, W. S.	Newtonville	1867
Andrus, A.	Westerville	1872
Applegate, Fred. C.	Windham	1859
Armstrong, T. H.	Powhatan Point	1862
Ayres, J. H.	Urbana	1876
Bailey, J. S.	Freeport	1873
Ball, A.	Zanesville	1848
Baker, Norman,	Lucas	1858
Ballinger, Wm. J.	Plain City	1864
Barker, Wm.	Attica	1876
Banning, J. C.	Round House	1876
Bartholow, Roberts,	Cincinnati	1869
Bartlett, E. P.	Genoa	1874
Beach, C. H.	Wellington	1868
Beach, T. D.	Alton	1874
Beach, J. N.	West Jefferson	1859
Beach, A. J.	Belleville	1863
Belding, Alvin,	Ravenna	1853
Bell, E. R.	Ripley	1871

NAME.	P. O. ADDRESS.	ADMITTED.
Bell, A. E.	Zanesville	1855
Beagrand, Pierce,	Fremont	1853
Besse, H.	Delaware	1868
Battles, W. S.	Shreve	1858
Berlin, C. T.	Wapakoneta	1868
Bennett, P. C.	Garrettsville	1870
Bennet, John,	Cleveland	1869
Beardsley, C. E.	Ottawa	1869
Bertolett, W. J.	Shreve	1869
Bertolett, J. B.	Letonia	1870
Bertolett, H. A.	Washingtonville	1870
Berger, S. H	Toledo	1874
Beverly, P. F.	Westerville	1862
Bishop, J. C.	Middleport	1873
Bishop, L. W.	Maineville	1871
Bishop, S. P.	Delta	1870
Bigney, P. M.	Cincinnati	1871
Bigelow, J. M.	Lancaster	1846
Bigelow, Asa,	Toledo	1874
Bing, J. P.	Portsmouth	1851
Bington, Joseph,	Williamstown, Va.	1876
Blizzard, S. R.	Huntsville	1860
Blymer, A.	Delaware	1868
Black, J. R.	Newark	1867
Bland, Jerome,	Poplar P. O.	1876
Blesch, P. E.	Columbus	1869
Bonner, Stephen,	Cincinnati	1847
Bond, J. W.	Toledo	1874
Boyd, G. M.	Xenia	1857
Bowers, E. D.	Columbus	1861
Boerstler, G. W., Jr.	Lancaster	1870
Brockett, A. J.	Bristolville	1874
Brown, J. E.	McConnellsville	1873
Brown, A. M.	Cincinnati	1851
Brown, S. H.	Dennison	1876
Brown, J. C.	Urbana	1863
Brown, J. A.	DeGraff	1860
Brook, G. W.	Ellsworth	1858
Brooks, J. H.	Brownsville	1854
Bruce, A. G.	Clarksfield	1870

NAME.	P. O. ADDRESS.	ADMITTED.
Bramble, D. D.	Cincinnati	1870
Bryson, C. C.	Millersport	1871
Brainard, A. C.	Orangeville	1870
Brainard, H. C.	Cleveland	1870
Bryant, W. G.	Springfield	1871
Bracken, W. C.	Jersey	1869
Brayton, A.	Cary	1859
Brellen, Joseph,	Grove City	1856
Bricker, W. R.	Shelby	1848
Brinkerhoof, D. H.	Fremont	1853
Buckner, J. H.	Cincinnati	1863
Buckingham, E. M.	Springfield	1855
Buckingham, E. V. B.	Centerton	1874
Burr, J. N.	Mount Vernon	1853
Bunce, Wm.	Oberlin	1864
Butler, G. W.	Columbus	1869
Butler, Geo. O.	Cleveland	1870
Belts, Mrs. Helen L.	Youngstown	1875
Brooks, Mrs. S.	Akron	1875
Baldwin, J. F.	Columbus	1875
Campbell, John,	Uniontown	1855
Campbell, J.	Dennison	1876
Campbell, W. H.	Vanceburg, Ky.	1871
Caruthers, John A.	Killbourne	1859
Caldwell, W. W.	Hamilton	1874
Cadwallader, Rowland,	Findlay	1862
Carmichael, W. A.	Loveland	1871
Cassat, M.	Cincinnati	1870
Carson, Wm.	Cincinnati	1871
Carson, W. B.	McComb	1874
Carrick, A. L.	Cincinnati	1871
Chase, B. S.	Akron	1870
Chase, James L.	Toledo	1874
Chamberlain, D. P.	Toledo	1874
Cherry, Wm.	Toledo	1874
Chisholm, J. W.	Mt. Perry	1873
Clark, Henry P.	Ashland	1862
Clark, John H.	Dayton	1869
Clark, M. S.	Mahoning Co.	1876
Clason, Thos. S.	Bellefontaine	1865

NAME.	P. O. ADDRESS.	ADMITTED.
Cotton, J. D.	Marietta	1852
Cotton, D. B.	Portsmouth	1872
Cottle, L. A.	Maineville	1871
Coleman, David,	West Union	1872
Coble, D. W.	Westerville	1872
Courtwright, A. P.	Cincinnati	1871
Courtwright, G. S.	Lithopolis	1867
Conklin, W. J.	Dayton	1868
Conklin, H. S.	Sidney	1849
Conner, P. S.	Cincinnati	1868
Constant, W. S.	Delaware	1866
Coons, Israel A.	Middletown	1853
Corson, John,	Middletown	1866
Comegys, C. G.	Cincinnati	1871
Combs, J. S.	Owensville	1865
Corwell, H. G.	Youngstown	1874
Corey, John M.	Fremont	1874
Coldham, James,	Toledo	1874
Casgrove, Thos.	Sylvania	1875
Crafts, John M.	Mantua, Portage Co.	1874
Craig, B. W.	Mansfield	1874
Culver, J. F.	Belpre	1874
Cuykendall, M. C.	Bucyrus	1874
Cutler, E. J.	Cleveland	1870
Cutler, James,	Bell Point	1864
Curry, J. H.	Toledo	1876
Cushing, H. K.	Cleveland	1857
Culbertson, Howard	Zanesville	ʼ1855
Coulson, E. G.	Pennsville	1875
Coleman, N. R.	Harrisville	1875
Chapman, W. C.	Toledo	1875
Cooney, H.	Bryon	1875
Cake, W. M.	West Independence	1875
Dawson, W. W.	Cincinnati	1853
Davis, John,	Dayton	1853
Davis, John,	Cincinnati	1854
Davis, O. E.	Cincinnati	1871
Davis, Wm. B.	Cincinnati	1865
Davis, T. D.	Dayton	1872
Dandridge, A. S.	Cincinnati	1854

NAME.	P. O. ADDRESS.	ADMITTED.
Dandridge, N. P. . .	Cincinnati . .	1871
Darwin, Henry W. .	Gettysburg .	1859
Dalby, Isaac N. . .	Cleveland . .	1870
Day, E. A. . .		1871
Dew, J. S. . . .	Trimble . .	1873
Denning, R. M. .	Columbus .	1851
Dean, Geo. A. . .	McComb . .	1874
Duncan, James A. .	Toledo . .	1874
Denman, M. N. . .	West Unity .	1874
Donahoe; H. J. .	Sandusky . .	1854
Douglass, W. W. . .	Toledo . .	1874
Downs, Samuel, . .	Waterville . .	1876
Drake, I. L. . .	Lebanon . .	1859
Drury, Wm. H. . .	Columbus . .	1859
Dunlap, Alexander, .	Springfield .	1854
Dunlap, A. S. . .	Dayton . .	1868
Dunlap, C. W. . .	Springfield .	1869
Dunham, J. M. . .	Columbus . . .	1873
Davy, R. B. . .	Cincinnati .	1875
Ebright, L. S. . .	Wadsworth . .	1870
Eckman, Hiram, .	Tuscarawas .	1869
Edwards, J. D. . .	Xenia . . .	1867
Edwards, Tom O., Jr.	Lancaster .	1873
Ellis, A. N. . .	Lockland . .	1868
Ellsberry, W. W. .	Georgetown .	1874
Erwin, R. W. . .	Bay City, Michigan	1872
Estep, William, .	Lloydsville .	1852
Everhard, N S. . .	Wadsworth . .	1870
Ewing, James, . .	Hebrun . .	1875
Farrell, T. J. . .	Columbus . .	1873
Falconer, Cyrus, .	Hamilton .	1854
Fenneberg, Gustavus .	Toledo . .	1874
Firmin, F. W. . .	Findlay . .	1874
Fisher, P. Q. . .	Nashport . .	1873
Fisher, W. S. . .	Bridgeport . .	1876
Firestone, J. L. .	Salem . .	1870
Firestone, L. . .	Wooster . .	1852
Finch, S. F. . .	Green Springs .	1857
Finch, C. M. . .	Portsmouth . .	1869
Forbes, S F. . .	Toledo . .	1856

NAME.	P. O. ADDRESS.	ADMITTED.
Ford, J. B.	Norwalk	1876
Follett, Alfred,	Granville	1864
Foster, Nathaniel,	Cincinnati	1854
Fowler, S. W.	Delaware	1873
Frizzell, W. A.	Freestone	1872
Frankenberg, O.	Columbus	1873
Franklin, G. S.	Chillicothe	1876
Fuller, A. B.	Loudonville	1868
Fuller, S. W.	Bellefontaine	1853
Fisher, A. W.	Toledo	1875
Gardner, G. W.	Harrisburg	1873
Gay, N.	Columbus	1848
Gabriel, J. F.	Piqua	1856
Galpin, Loman,	Milan	1857
Gawne, A. J.	Cleveland	1870
Galer, Frank M.	De Graff	1874
Galbraith, E. J.	Frankfort	1876
Gerwe, F. A. J.	Cincinnati	1854
Gillett, Bartley,	Springfield	1849
Gilchrist, R. S.	De Graff	1856
Gilliam, D. L.	Nelsonville	1873
Gibson, Richard McD.	Tiffin	1871
Gordon, T. W.	Georgetown	1849
Goble, P.	Worthington	1849
Gotwald, A. G.	Dayton	1854
Gonsaulis, C.	Sparta	1863
Goldrick, Wm.	Delaware	1868
Gould, D. T.	Cleveland	1870
Goodlove, Wm.	Monterey	1874
Goodson, J. W.	Bellevue	1874
Green, J. W.	Fairfield	1853
Green, J. H.	Troy	1871
Gray, S. S.	Piqua	1867
Graefe, Wm.	Sandusky City	1874
Gundry, Richard,	Athens	1856
Guerin, Z. F.	Columbus	1856
Guyttard, F.	New Bedford	1870
Guthrie, James W.	Wooster	1870
Glenn, Mrs. G. C.	Akron	1875
Graefe, Phillip,	Sandusky	1875

NAME.	P. O. ADDRESS.	ADMITTED.
Greenamyer, P. S.	Smithville	1875
Grissell, E.	Salem	1876
Harley, L. G.	Dalton	1853
Hamilton, J. W.	Columbus	1849
Hart, B. F.	Marietta	1854
Harmon, Julian,	Warren	1857
Hall, W. E.	Fayetteville	1859
Hall, N.	Cumminsville	1871
Hall, J. M.	Fayetteville	1871
Hall, C. B.	Millersport	1872
Hall, Camillus,	Burlington	1872
Hadley, Edwin,	Richmond	1865
Hazzard, J. S. R.	Springfield	1867
Harrison, Eugene B.	Napoleon	1869
Halderman, D.	Columbus	1869
Hadlock, J. W.	Cincinnati	1871
Hague, J. H.	Nashville	1874
Hartman, S. Duff,	Tippecanoe City	1874
Hathaway, Calvin,	Edgerton	1874
Hathaway, Harrison,	Weaver's Corners	1874
Helbish, F. S.	Green Springs	1876
Helmick, S. C.	Commercial Point	1873
Helmick, J.	Harrisburg	1849
Henderson, J. P.	Newville	1850
Henderson, D. W.	Marysville	1856
Henderson, R. A.	Upper Sandusky	1865
Hendrickson, Hugh,	Lewis Center	1868
Herrick, H. J.	Cleveland	1865
Herrick, L. C.	Woodstock	1871
Heuston, R. C.	Oxford	1868
Heighway, A. E.	Cincinnati	1870
Hill, G. W.	Ashland	1873
Hill, E. L.	Oxford	1857
Hill, N. S.	Neville	1866
Hill, H.	West Alexandria	1867
Hildreth, C. C.	Zanesville	1853
Hitchcock, James,	Port Clinton	1857
Higgins, C. W.	Big Plain	1869
Hiner, S. B.	Lima	1874
Hines, Isaac N.	Cleveland	1874

NAME.	P. O. ADDRESS.	ADMITTED.
Holston, J. G. F., Jr.	Zanesville	1873
Hoover, T. C.	Bellaire City	1873
Howard, E. W.	Akron	1852
Holston, J. G. F.	Zanesville	1850
Hopkins, D. O.	St. Paris	1866
Hough, J. B.	Ridgeville	1869
Houghton, J. W.	Wellington	1870
Hobson, J. F.	Newburg	1870
Hoff, J. W.	Pomeroy	1872
Holdt, George,	Cincinnati	1871
Hoege, Geo. L.	Fostoria	1874
Hohly, Frederick,	Toledo	1874
Huestis, Isaac,	Chester Hill	1869
Hughes, E. E.	Thurman	1873
Hubbard, J. C.	Ashtabula	1856
Hunt, A. H.	Blackleyville	1868
Hurd, A.	Findlay	1870
Huggins, R. D.	West Alexandria	1871
Hyatt, E. H.	Delaware	1862
Hyde, Wm.	Wauseon	1871
Hale, R. W.	Fostoria	1875
Hanford, F. A.	Akron	1875
Hard, E. G.	Medina	1875
Hovey, A. B.	Tiffin	1875
Holliday, B. W.	Cleveland	1875
Hagus, H. P.	Ravenna	1875
Hirter, Carl,	Sandusky	1875
Haugh, W. S.	Cuyahoga Falls	1875
Isham, A. B.	Walnut Hills, Cin.	1871
Jacoby, F.	Columbus	1873
Jacobs, W. C.	Akron	1866
Jenner, A. E.	Crestline	1866
Jennings, E.	Dayton	1867
Jennings, J. D.	Sonora	1869
Jewett, W. H.	Hilliard	1869
Jewett, M.	Middlebury	1870
Jewett, H. S.	Dayton	1871
Jones, T. W.	Columbus	1847
Jones, R. E.	Gomer	1863
Jones, A. B.	Portsmouth	1868

NAME.	P. O. ADDRESS.	ADMITTED.
Jones, W. H.	Cleveland	1868
Jones, L. M.	West Liberty	1869
Jones, W. W.	Toledo	1849
Jones, J. D.	Newburg	1870
Jones, N. M.	Cleveland	1870
Jones, Philo E.	Wauseon	1874
Jobes, J. A.	German, Darke Co.	1870
Joseph, A. P.	Fairmont	1862
Junkens, M. W.	Bellaire	1859
Kay, Isaac,	Springfield	1853
Keever, M. H.	Ridgeville	1850
Kennedy, J. C.	Batavia	1854
Keyt, A. T.	Walnut Hills, Cin.	1850
Kelley, H. R.	Galion	1868
Kemp, J. D.	Dayton	1868
Kemper, And. C.	Cincinnati	1871
Kearney, T. H.	Cincinnati	1871
Kendig, E. V.	Haynesville	1874
Kincaid, W. P.	New Richmond	1854
Kingham, Joseph,	Port Clinton	1875
Kinnaman, J. W.	Ashland	1870
Kirby, Jacob,	Hillsboro	1871
Kitchen, B. F.	Clay Post Office	1872
Kitchen, H. W.	Cleveland	1874
Kirkley, Cyrus A.	Toledo	1874
Knowlton, A. P.	Olmstead Falls	1870
Knox, C. E.	Bellaire	1875
Kury, ——	Bellaire	1875
Laisy, Jacob,	Cleveland	1874
Lawless, J. T.	Toledo	1874
Landon, C. P.	Westerville	1851
Lamme, W. H.	Xenia	1853
Lane, E. S.	Sandusky	1853
Larimore, F. C.	Mt. Vernon	1871
Larimore, James,	Newark	1875
Lang, E. R.	Portsmouth	1871
Leonard, B. B.	West Liberty	1854
Leonhard, C. S.	Ravenna	1865
Lewis, Edward C.	Canal Dover	1870
Lewis, W. C.	Rushville	1869

15

NAME.	P. O. ADDRESS.	ADMITTED.
Lewis, D.	New Haven	1848
Lee, E. B.	Garrettsville	1870
Little, J. A.	Delaware	1868
Linskey, C. H.	Put-in-Bay	1876
Loving, S.	Columbus	1858
Longfellow, A. J.	Fostoria	1861
Longworth, W. N.	Van Wert	1866
Loller, W. B.	Nashville	1864
Lord, J. M.	Chesterville	1868
Logan, W. M.	Cincinnati	1871
Lucky, J. B.	Elmore	1874
Luddington, H.	Cincinnati	1871
Ludlow, J.	Cincinnati	1871
Lyman, C. N.	Wadsworth	1852
Longworth, L. R.	Cincinnati	1875
Long, J. W.	Bryan	1875
Mahlman, H. A.	Columbus	1869
Mahlman, C. H. W.	Columbus	1859
Matchett, W. H.	Greenville	1862
Maynard, A.	Cleveland	1863
Mack, John,	Shelby	1853
McBeth, J. C.	Galion	1858
McBride, Alexander,	Berea	1865
McCann,	Napoleon	1875
McCarty, Oliver.	Polk	1858
McCasky, H.	Felicity	1868
McCurdy, John,	Youngstown	1870
McCollom, E. J.	Tiffin	1871
McClure, James,	Marietta	1866
McClurg, John,	Center Village	1863
McCullough, J. G.	Bealsville	1868
McCullough, A. M. F.	Bealsville	1874
McDermott, C.	Dayton	1857
McDowell, W. J.	Portsmouth	1872
McEbright, Thomas G.	Akron	1866
McElwe, S.	New Castle	1866
McFarland, J. A.	Tiffin	1850
McGraw, Aaron,	Burton	1869
McGuire, J.	Norwalk	1870
McKean, Wm.	Mount Hope	1870

NAME.	P. O. ADDRESS.	ADMITTED.
McKinley, C. G.	Sunbury	1866
McKenna, L. F.	Junction City	1878
McKechnie	Wilmington	1876
McLaughlin, A. C.	Tremont	1852
McLaughlin, R.	Butler	1869
McNally, Thomas,	Chillicothe	1858
McNeely, J. S.	Hamilton	1867
McMillan, Alex.	Genoa	1875
McMann, E. W.	Napoleon	1875
McConnelly, C. M.	Vermillion	1875
McClellan, R. M.	Xenia	1875
Mann, H. L.	Wapakoneta	1875
Mead, M. L.	Cleveland	1875
Merrell, A. E.	Vermillion	1876
Musgrove, W. A.	Urbana	1875
Metcalf, C. T.	Warren	1870
Mendenhall, J. W.	Marathon	1871
Metzler, A. S.	Buena Vista	1874
Myers, Benj.	Ashland	1874
Minor, T. C.	Cincinnati	1878
Miller, A. C.	Orrville	1868
Miller, Thomas V.	Columbus	1869
Miller, T. C.	Cleveland	1870
Miller, C. A.	Orrville	1871
Miles, A. J.	Cincinnati	1869
Mitchell, George,	Mansfield	1868
Moe, L. W.	Ottawa	1860
Monahan, A. B.	Jackson	1872
Moore, W. C.	Wooster	1872
Moore, William,	New Lisbon	1865
Moore, Eugene L.	Moscow	1868
Moore, E.	Warren	1868
Moore, A. C.	Aurora	1869
Moore, James,	Jackson	1872
Morey, J. J.		1871
Morris, F. B.	Kent	1869
Morris, Jonathan,		1873
Morse, D. A.		1872
Morgan, J. B.		1873
Morgan, L. D.		1872

NAME.	P. O. ADDRESS.	ADMITTED.
Mounts, J. L.	Morrow	1860
Mouser, J. A.	LaRue	1870
Murphy, J. A.	Cincinnati	1872
Muscroft, C. S.	Cincinnati :	1854
Mussy, W. H.	Cincinnati	1854
Mullen, T. J.	New Richmond	1855
Murray, L. S.	Medina	1870
Murbach, A. J.	Archibald	1874
Nash, W. H. H.	Quaker Bottoms	1874
Naw, J. H.	Carroll	1873
Neal, T. L.	Dayton	1863
Neil, Alexander,	Columbus	1868
Nicholson, W. H.	Cleveland	1853
Noble, C. D.	Oberlin	1870
Noble, David,	Hillsboro	1860
Nolan, J. G.	Toledo	1874
Norman, Frank,	Columbus	1873
Nourse, J. D.	Reynoldsburg	1873
Nunemaker, N. B.	Athens	1875
Orr, G. B.	Cincinnati	1871
Owsley, J. B.	Jacksonburg	1871
Osborn, A. S.	Peru	1875
Paige, W. F.	Johnstown	1864
Palmer, C. D.	Cincinnati	1871
Patterson, A. V.	Mansfield	1861
Patterson, Wilson S.	New Lexington	1874
Pearce, Enoch, Jr.	Steubenville	1859
Pearce, H. C.	Urbana	1867
Pearce, L. E.	Cable	1869
Peck, W. L.	College Hill	1853
Peck, W. V.	New Richmond	1872
Perrin, James,	Cleveland	1870
Phillips, H. W.	Kenton	1866
Pixley, S. M.	Portsmouth	1873
Pixley, Sumner,	Cleveland	1870
Pollock, Calvin,	Donnelsville	1873
Pomerene, P. P.	Berlin	1870
Pomerine, Joel,	Millersburg	1858
Pomeroy, O.	Chardon	1869
Potter, J. B.	Canal Winchester	1847

NAME.	P. O. ADDRESS.	ADMITTED.
Pooley, J. H.	Columbus	1876
Pratt, E. B.	Mount Sterling	1869
Price, Joseph,	Randolph	1852
Preston, J. C.	Brunswick	1857
Priest, Jonathan,	Toledo	1874
Primrose, J. P.	Nelsonville	1872
Pullen, G. W.	Logan	1864
Pape, Leopold,	Sandusky	1875
Quinn, J. J.	Cincinnati	1875
Ralston, D. H.	Granville	1864
Rathbun, C.	Salem	1860
Rankin, A. H.	Sandusky	1870
Randall, R.	Bath	1870
Raymond, B.	Lancaster	1860
Reamy, T. A.	Cincinnati	1855
Reed, N. C.	Columbus	1873
Reed, C. H.	Toledo	1878
Reed, A. B.	Brooklyn Village	1870
Reed, A. N.	Norwalk	1870
Reed, R. C. S.	Jones' Station	1867
Reed, William,	Iberia	1865
Reed, C. R.	Middleport	1864
Reed, C. A. Lee,	Cincinnati	1874
Reeve, J. C.	Dayton	1861
Reid, J. L.	Van Wert	1874
Reed, J. T.	Massillon	1875
Ridenour, A. W.	Massillon	1875
Ringham, J.	Port Clinton	1875
Riggs, John U.	Bryan	1873
Rice, J. B.	Fremont	1868
Ridenour, W. T.	Toledo	1870
Rives, Landon,	Cincinnati	1853
Robb, Andrew,	Blanchester	1859
Robertson, Charles,	McConnellsville	1849
Robinson, J. D.	Wooster	1856
Robinson, J. N.	Medina	1856
Robb, M.		1871
Rodgers, J. H.	Springfield	1859
Rogers, Robert,	Springfield	1847
Rogers, J. G.	New Richmond	1853

NAME.	P. O. ADDRESS.	ADMITTED.
Roots, W. Y.	Milford Center	1869
Root, H. A.	Toledo	1874
Root, E. B.	Painsville	1874
Ropp, W. T.	Delaware	1869
Rosenfeldt, A.	Cincinnati	1871
Russell, J. W.	Mt. Vernon	1848
Russell, I. W.	Mt. Vernon	1870
Runyon, ——	West Unity	1874
Salisbury, J. N.	Russellville	1872
Saylor, Will,	Gratis	1871
Scarf, W. D.	Bellefontaine	1855
Schwab, Louis,	Portsmouth	1872
Scoville, S. S.	Lebanon	1859
Schueller, J. B.	Columbus	1869
Scott, A. J.	Loudenville	1870
Scott, Xenophen C.	Cleveland	1874
Scott, W. J.	Cleveland	1855
Schnetzler, H. M.	Toledo	1874
Seaton, A. M.	Medway	1869
Seely, W. W.	Cincinnati	1871
Seeds, R. Z.	Hilliard	1873
Seldon, O. G.	Shanesville	1851
Seldon, Robert,	Shanesville	1870
Sensaman, H.	Tremont	1871
Sellers, A.	Lebanon	1867
Severance, R. A.	Bellevue	1874
Shepherd, W. E. W.	Nelsonville	1873
Shepherd, W. W.	Hillsboro	1871
Shackelton, E. L.	St. Mary's	1871
Sherman, A. M.	Kent	1870
Shoemaker, J. M.	Napoleon	1869
Sharp, W. T.	Middleburg	1853
Shouse, B. A.	Berne	1868
Shively, J. W.	Massillon	1858
Sinnet, E.	Granville	1850
Silver, D. R.	Sidney	1870
Sidwell, N. H.	Wilmington	1871
Slocum, Charles,	Defiance	1874
Smith, S. D.	Lockington	1874
Smith, C. T.	Middleport	1873

NAME.	P. O. ADDRESS.	ADMITTED.
Smith, J. H.	Delaware	1873
Smith, J. W.	Wellington	1863
Smith, Harry,	Mt. Vernon	1869
Smith, D. B.	Cleveland	1870
Smith, James,	Clarington	1876
Snodgrass, J. M.	Ostrander	1871
Snyder, D. J.	Scio	1850
Southard, J. M.	Marysville	1860
Sparrow, T. R.	Columbus	1873
Spencer, B. T.	Newark	1873
Spees, S. J.	Hillsboro	1863
Sprague, James,	London	1866
Speece, N. V.	Quincy	1870
Stein, Geo. T.	Columbus	1873
Stephenson, Y.	Georgetown	1872
Stephenson, J. H.	Leesville	1860
Stevenson, A. G.	Richmond	1856
Stark, W.	Cincinnati	1871
Stevens, E. B.	Syracuse, N. Y.	1853
Stillwell, Thomas,	Fremont	1857
Stanley, E.	Sandusky	1870
Stansell, J. A.	Forest	1866
Stockstill, J. W.	New Carlisle	1867
'Stewart, J. W.	Dayton	1868
Stewart, S. H.	Columbus	1869
Steeley, H. G.	Sidney	1869
Stanton, Byron,	Cincinnati	1871
Sweeney, R. L.	Marion	1859
Sykes, W. H.	Plymouth	1870
Smith, W. K.	Deersville	1875
Sauer, Mrs. P. B.	Napoleon	1875
Tagert, E. Curtis,	Hilliard	1871
Tauber, B.	Cincinnati	1876
Taylor, James, L.	Wheelersburg	1872
Taylor, W. H.	Cincinnati	1874
Terry, C. A.	Cleveland	1870
Thompson, J. C.	South Bloomfield	1848
Thompson, J. B.	Columbus	1846
Thompson, W. R.	Vandalia	1871
Thorn, S. S.	Toledo	1873

NAME.	P. O. ADDRESS.	ADMITTED.
Thorn, E.	Yellow Springs	1867
Thornton, W. P.	Cincinnati	1871
Thurston, R. C.	Oxford	1868
Tipton, R. H.	Darbyville	1853
Tichenor, E. J.	Lebanon	1869
Titus, A.	Wheelersburg	1871
Treon, John,	Miamisburg	1853
Turney, S. D.	Circleville	1856
Tupper, C. E.	Ottawa	1874
Underwood, A. H.	London	1869
Underwood, W. J.	Akron	1869
Underhill, J. W.	Cincinnati	1874
Vail, D. W.	New Haven	1874
Vanatta, E.	Fultonham	1855
Vance, D. M.	Urbana	1876
Vandervort, J. W.	Harveysburg	1864
Vattier, J. L.	Cincinnati	1850
Vaughters, Thomas G.	Portsmouth	1872
Voorhees, S. R.	Mason	1873
Waddick, J. M.	Toledo	1873
Waddle, Thomas,	Toledo	1874
Wade, D. E.	Cincinnati	1854
Wagenhals, P. M.	Columbus	1869
Waggoner, Joseph,	Ravenna	1870
Walton, George E.	Cincinnati	1871
Ward, C. S.	Warren	1875
Watt, William,	Kenton	1870
Wallace, J. H.	Smithville	1870
Warren, Guy,	Garrettsville	1870
Warren, J. A.	Wheelersburg	1872
Waterman, H. C.	Middleport	1868
Weber, G. C. E.	Cleveland	1857
Webster, E. M.	Kingsview	1876
Welsh, J. W.	Deersville	1873
Welsh, B. F.	London	1859
Weed, Frank J.	Cleveland	1870
Weaver, J. M.	Dayton	1865
Westbrock, A. E.	Ashley	1872
Wheaton, J. M.	Columbus	1869
White, J. H.	Delaware	1866

NAME.	P. O. ADDRESS.	ADMITTED.
Whitmar, Joel E.	Mount Hope	1874
Whiting, L. M.	Canton	1870
Whittaker, J. T.	Cincinnati	1871
Whitehead, A. M.	Springfield	1873
Wilson, J. L.	Greenfield	1871
Wilson, Samuel,	Wooster	1854
Wilson, Albert,	Sidney	1854
Wilson, W. F.	Ironton	1856
Wilson, W. H.	Greenfield	1865
Wilson, C. M.	Miami Springs	1872
Wilson, D. C.	Ironton	1872
Wise, S. P.	Millersburg	1875
Willard, G. P.	Tiffin	1875
Williams, A. S.	Fostoria	1852
Williams, E.	Cincinnati	1856
Williams, T. B.	Delaware	1860
Williams, D. S.	West Independence	1868
Williams, A. D.	Cincinnati	1868
Williams, A. Lee,	North Lewisburg	1871
Wilkins, John A.	Delta	1874
Wilbur, A. M.	West Unity	1874
Wirth, R.	Columbus	1865
Willis, P. A.	Bellepoint	1868
Willis, T. A.	Bellepoint	1868
Wiggins, C. W.	Big Plain	1869
Wood, D. B.	Warren	1852
Wood, John R.	Warren	1871
Wood, D. M.	Warren	1875
Woods, J. T.	Toledo	1862
Woodbridge, T.	Youngstown	1870
Woodward, Charles,*	Cincinnati	1851
Woodward, Warren,	Cincinnati	1871
Woodruff, L.	Alton	1867
Wolfley, W. J.	Columbus	1873
Worthington, A. T. C.	Middletown	1871
Wright, M. B.	Cincinnati	1852
Wylie, A. N.	Ripley	1866
Wylie, J. L.	Ripley	1872
West, T. J.	Melmore	1875
Yates, Porter,	Green Spring	1875

16   *Died 1874.

Honorary Members.

Dr. Awl, Columbus.
M. J. Bailey, M. D., New York City.
J. H. Brower, M. D., Lawrenceburg, Indiana.
J. C. Blackburn, M. D., Covington, Kentucky.
G. W. Boerstler,* M. D., Lancaster, Ohio.
P. Beeman, M. D., Sidney, Ohio.
Wm. Brodie, President, Michigan State Medical Society.
Professor H. H. Childs, Pittsfield, Massachusetts.
H. Conant, M. D., Maumee City.
G. B. Guthrie, M. D., New York City.
M. M. Harding, M. D., Indiana.
J. L. Hayes, M. D., Philadelphia, Pennsylvania.
R. E. Houghton, M. D., Richmond, Ind.
S. P. Hunt, M. D., Sterling, Illinois.
G. S. B. Hempstead, M. D., Portsmouth, Ohio.
E. W. Jenks, Ex-President, Michigan State Med. Society.
Professor J. Knight, New Haven, Connecticut.
J. M. Kitchen, M. D., Indianapolis, Indiana.
Jared P. Kirtland, Cleveland.
John Kerr, Canton, China.
Professor Charles A. Lee,* New York City.
W. B. Lyons, M. D., Huntington, Indiana.
R. R. McIlvaine, M. D., New York City.
Professor R. D. Mussey,* Cincinnati, Ohio.
J. F. Noyes, Delegate, Michigan State Medical Society.
Professor Willard Parker, New York.
J. M. Stevenson, M. D., Pennsylvania.
H. K. Steele, M. D., Denver, Colorado.
Geo. Sutton, M. D., Aurora, Indiana.
Professor Wm. Tully,* New Haven, Connecticut.
Robert Thompson,* M. D., Columbus, Ohio.

*Deceased.

Honorary and Corresponding Members.

Professor Ferdinand Hebra, Vienna, Austria.

Professor Isidor Neumann, Vienna, Austria.

Professor Hermann Widerhofer, Vienna, Austria.

Professor Carl Sigmund, Vienna, Austria.

Professor Hermann Zeissl, Vienna, Austria.

Professor Ed. C. Seaton, Medical Inspector of the Privy Council, London, England.

Professor M. Jules Guerin, Member Imperial Academy of Medicine, Paris, France.

Milton Keynes UK
Ingram Content Group UK Ltd.
UKHW040139160224
437928UK00003B/34